'You *will* marry me, just as everything has been arranged already,' he countered. 'You *will* accept with grace anything I choose to bestow on you, and you will *not* go back to work.'

Lizzy swung to face him and was shocked by the kick she received low in her gut because he was so— 'Y-you can't just slot me into Bianca's place just like that,' she fed, over what her body was trying to make her feel. 'The authorities won't allow it!'

'At the risk of sounding boringly repetitive, money talks.'

Money talks. And so it did. 'I think I hate you,' she whispered.

'Nevertheless you will take up Bianca's place with pride and dignity, and fool the world into thinking it was you and I who discovered we couldn't live without each other. And you will *not* pay me back with anything other than with our first child, seeded in your womb. With that goal in mind you will come to our marriage bed with warmth and honesty—which means you will not fight against what we both desire.'

Michelle Reid grew up on the southern edges of Manchester, the youngest in a family of five lively children. Now she lives in the beautiful county of Cheshire, with her busy executive husband and two grown-up daughters. She loves reading, the ballet, and playing tennis when she gets the chance. She hates cooking, cleaning, and despises ironing! Sleep she can do without, and produces some of her best written work during the early hours of the morning.

Recent titles by the same author:

THE MARKONOS BRIDE
THE ITALIAN'S FUTURE BRIDE

THE DE SANTIS MARRIAGE

BY
MICHELLE REID

MILLS & BOON
Pure reading pleasure

First published in Great Britain 2008
Harlequin Mills & Boon Limited,
Eton House, 18-24 Paradise Road, Richmond, Surrey TW9 1SR

© Michelle Reid 2008

ISBN: 978 0 263 20318 9

Set in Times Roman 10½ on 12¾ pt
07-0708-51252

Printed and bound in Great Britain
by Antony Rowe Ltd, Chippenham, Wiltshire

THE DE SANTIS MARRIAGE

CHAPTER ONE

THE WHOLE pre-wedding party thing was revving up like a gigantic engine and Lizzy had never felt less like partying in her entire life.

Now a night at La Scala, dear God, she thought heavily. For here she stood surrounded by luxury in this posh Milan hotel suite, about to put on a posh designer dress that must have cost more money than she dared let herself think about, so she could look the part for a posh gala evening spent at La Scala, while back home in England the family business was about to go under taking everything they owned along with it.

She had not wanted to come to her best friend's wedding but her father had insisted. Her brother Matthew had gone a whole step further and become really angry. 'Don't be stupid,' he'd snapped at her. 'Do you want Dad to feel worse than he already does about this mess? Go to Bianca's wedding as planned,' he'd instructed, 'and while you're there wish her all the damn best from me with her super-rich catch.'

It had been said with such bite it made Lizzy wince to recall him saying it. Matthew was never going to forgive her best friend for falling in love with another man.

Then Bianca and her parents had put even more pressure on her to come to Milan and in the end it had been easier to give in and do what everyone wanted her to do when all *she'd* wanted to do was to be at her father's side supporting him.

But instead she had to shimmy into this dress, Lizzy told herself, puffing back an unruly curl when it flopped across one eye as she settled the straps onto her shoulders then turned to the mirror to check out the finished effect.

What she saw reflected back at her sent instant horror pouring into her expressive face. The dress was way too clingy in all the wrong places and the silver-grey colour looked awful against her pale skin! And it was not for the first time in her twenty-two years that she wished with all her heart that she were a delicate and sweet fine-boned brunette like Bianca.

But she wasn't. She was a long curvy redhead with an unruly long mop of glossy chestnut curls that just refused to stay confined no matter how much torture she put herself through in an effort to pin them up. Add skin so startlingly white it looked dreadful against the silver-threaded grey silk and it was like looking at a ghost!

When Bianca had bought the dress a couple of months ago to wear to her betrothal party she'd looked fabulous in it— pure sensation on legs. Yesterday she'd tossed it at Lizzy in disgust. 'I don't know why I bought it. I hate the colour. The length is not right and my boobs don't fill it.'

Well, there was no chance of that problem here, Lizzy thought, small white teeth biting down into her full bottom lip as she hitched the tightly fitted basque top further up the pale plump slopes of breasts and grimly thanked the boning in the bodice for helping it to stay put.

The rest, she saw on second inspection, didn't cling quite as badly as she'd first thought it did and—Face it, Lizzy, she then told herself firmly, beggars cannot be choosers, girl, so you should—

The sudden knock sounding at her suite door diverted her attention. 'Are you ready, Elizabeth?' Bianca's mother called out. 'We must not be late for La Scala.'

Certainly not, Lizzy thought dryly. 'Just one more minute!' she called back.

La Scala waited for no man, not even the higher echelons of Italian society she was about to mingle with, she mocked as she slid her feet into a pair of high slender heeled silver mules, then turned to apply a coating of clear gloss to her lips. She refused point-blank to use the seduction red colour Bianca had supplied along with the dress.

Standing back to give her reflection the final once-over, she suddenly found the humour in standing here in her ill-fitting borrowed feathers and laughed for the first time in weeks. All she needed now was for her best friend to toss her that fabulous diamond ring her betrothed had presented her with and she'd be sorted. All family debts paid via the first pawn brokerage she could find.

But Bianca wasn't quite that giving—not that Lizzy resented her for that. Bianca Moreno had been her closest friend since the day they had both found themselves stuck in the same strict English boarding-school feeling like a pair of aliens dropped in there from outer space. Bianca had come to the school directly from a carefree lifestyle in Sydney with her Italian born parents. They'd gone from ordinary to mega-rich overnight when an uncle in England had died suddenly making Bianca's father the main beneficiary of the London based Moreno Inc.

Whereas Lizzy, well, she had been sent to the same school after her mother had caused a terrible scandal by having an affair with their local, very married MP. She had been so mercilessly teased and bullied at her old school about the affair that her father had decided to remove her from the situation by placing her in a school hundreds of miles away from the fuss.

Did it stop the teasing? No, it didn't. Did she tell her father that? No, she did not, because he'd already been too cast down by the scandal and the fact that their mother had walked out and left them taking with her what funds she could grab. So Bianca had become her close friend and confidante. They looked out for each other. Bianca was the black-haired black-eyed spitfire with a solid grounding in good Australian spunk and Lizzy the much quieter one with her natural spirit squashed by the bullies and a mother who'd never bothered to get in touch again after she'd walked out.

From the age of twelve to their present twenty-two, she and Bianca had rarely done anything without the other one knowing about it. Now her friend was about to marry into one of Italy's finest families and, despite not wanting to be here, Lizzy was ready to shelve her own worries and do whatever it was going to take to help make Bianca's wedding day next week absolutely perfect. It was Bianca's family who'd paid to bring her over here. They had provided her with everything from room and board to clothes to suit every glittering occasion, even if they were Bianca's cast-offs.

And she was grateful to them—she was, because she could not have afforded to come otherwise, no matter what her father had said. So here she was, one week into a two-week sabbatical from family troubles, joining in the partying run-up to Bianca's glossy marriage to her super-rich, super-sophisticated beau.

Luciano Genovese Marcelo De Santis, the thirty-four-year-old supreme head of the great and vast De Santis banking empire—Luc to his very close friends.

A tense little quiver made a sudden strike down Lizzy's front and in pure self-defence she snatched up a silvery silk crocheted snug from the bed and hurriedly tied it across her front while wishing to goodness that she didn't experience that same crazy tense quiver every time she let herself think about him.

He was strange—a truly intimidating mix of smoothly polished cool sophistication and lean, dark, sexy good looks. Bianca purred around him like a sleek kitten, which seemed to amuse him, but then Bianca was Italian and as a race of people they were like that, open and warm and more touchy-feely than the British—*her*, Lizzy thought, making the rueful distinction.

She'd never purred around any man and couldn't envisage ever wanting to—which made the way she quivered around Luc De Santis all the more disturbing to her peace of mind. He wasn't her type. He was too much of everything. Too big and tall, too lean and dark, too sexy and handsome—too crushingly cool and terrifyingly enigmatic, she decided as she hooked up her little silver beaded evening bag and headed for the door.

They'd met only once before she's come to Milan, in London several months ago at the private dinner Bianca's parents had held to introduce their future son-in-law to their English friends. Luc had come as such a shock to Lizzy that she had not been able to stop her eyes from constantly drifting in his direction because he was so far away from her idea of the kind of man her friend liked.

'What do you think?' Bianca asked her.

'Intimidating,' she said, because that evening was the first time the tense quiver had struck. 'He scares me to death.'

Bianca just laughed, but then she'd been laughing at everything. Happy—in love again—high as a kite. 'You'll get used to him, Lizzy,' she promised. 'He isn't nearly as awesome once you get to know him.'

Want to bet?

The next time she'd met him had been just a week ago, she recalled as she pushed the button to call the lift. He'd arrived here at the hotel looking for Bianca and found Lizzy standing in Reception having just arrived in Milan. He'd come over to her—of course, he would do with impeccable manners like his, she reasoned. Yet she still had not been able to stop the next quiver from making its strike.

He'd been angry that Bianca had not been at the airport to meet her—she'd seen the anger snap at his handsome dark features just before he'd blanked it out. When she'd said quickly that she hadn't been expecting to be met, his wide, sensual mouth had tugged into a telling flat line of disapproval.

Cool, calm and used to ordering people about, he'd then taken it upon himself to organise her arrival by making sure she had a nice suite of rooms and had even gone as far as to escort her up here to check the suite out for himself.

It had been the moment when his hand arrived at the base of her spine to politely usher her out of the lift that the next quiver had struck, shooting down her front like a flaming arrow and making her jerk away from him like a scalded cat, only to feel really foolish for doing it. Other than to send her one of his cool, steady looks, he'd let his hand fall to his side and thankfully made no comment.

Now here she was waiting to ride the same lift down to the mezzanine floor of the hotel where they were all gathering for drinks before they left. And if she'd avoided Luc De Santis like the absolute plague for the rest of this week Lizzy had a horrible suspicion she was not going to be able to do that tonight. The party was too small, the reserved boxes at La Scala too intimate. Her only hope was to manage to wangle it so she sat in a different box from him.

There was a mirror hanging on the wall by the lift and she diverted her attention to it to push the stray curl off her brow. It flopped back down again like a renegade. She should not have decided to pin it all up because it just wasn't going to behave, she predicted. But giving in and letting her hair hang down around her shoulders in a tumble of loose glossy corkscrews had only made her face look paler and her grey-green eyes look too big.

Like a frightened rabbit, she likened, wrinkling her nose as she gave the errant curl a teasing tug and watched it spring back into place again.

It had to be that precise moment that the lift doors slid open to reveal none other than the great man himself. Their eyes clashed for a startled second. Knowing he'd caught her pulling silly faces at her own reflection was enough to flood colour into Lizzy's cheeks.

'Oh,' she said, just too disconcerted to keep the dismay from sounding in her voice. 'Are you staying here too? I didn't know.'

Brief amusement lit the unusual gold colour of his eyes.

'Good evening, Elizabeth.' He always called her *Elizabeth* in that dark, deep, slightly lilting Italian accent of his. 'Are you coming in?'

Coming in—heck, she thought, letting her eyes run over him. He was wearing a conventional black silk dinner suit and was leaning casually against the rear wall of the lift, which should have helped to diminish his daunting height a little and that overwhelming sense of presence he always carried around everywhere with him—but didn't.

And the idea of stepping into a lift with him again did strange things to the nerves in her legs as she made them move. Finding a tense smile to flick his way, she then turned her back on him to watch as the doors closed them in.

Silence hummed as they waited. She could feel his eyes on her. Tension made her bite into the soft tissue of her inner lip.

'You look very beautiful tonight,' he murmured softly.

Lizzy had to fight down an inner wince. She knew what she looked like and she knew what he was seeing—the poor best friend decked out in the dress his betrothed had worn a couple of months ago at the party in London.

So, 'No I don't,' she therefore responded curtly.

It was a relief when the lift doors opened onto the elegant splendour of the hotel's mezzanine lounge bar. As she went to step out that hand arrived at the base of her spine again and this time she froze where she stood.

It just wasn't fair. Why did she always do something like this around him?

'Shall we?' he prompted smoothly.

Lizzy made herself walk forward, stingingly aware how his hand remained exactly where it was this time—as if he was taunting her silly reaction to him. The first person her eyes focused on was Bianca's mother, looking stunning in sparkling diamonds and unrelieved black.

'Oh, there you are, Lizzy,' she said, hurrying towards them with an anxious expression threatening to ruin her perfectly made-up face.

'Luciano,' she greeted, her dark eyes skimming warily over her future son-in-law's face before she returned them to Lizzy. 'I need a quick word with you, *cara*,' she begged.

'Of course.' Lizzy smiled, automatically softening her tone for this tiny, elegant woman whose nervous disposition made her worry about everything—and everything usually encom-passed her beautiful daughter. 'What's Bianca done now?' she asked.

Meant as a light tease, it was only when the man standing behind her said coolly, 'Nothing, I hope,' that she realised she'd spoken out of turn in front of him.

Sofia Moreno went pale. Lizzy got defensive on Bianca's *mamma*'s behalf because she'd noticed before that Sofia was not comfortable in Luc's presence.

'It was a joke,' she said sharply—too sharply by the sudden stillness she felt hit the man behind her and the flick of tension she felt play along the length of her spine until it gathered beneath the light pressure of his hand.

Next second he was leaning past her to brush kisses to Sofia's cheeks. Having to stand here, trapped between the hard warmth of his body and Sofia's delicate one, Lizzy felt a twinge of remorse because his gesture was so obviously offered as a gentle soothe to his future mother-in-law's frazzled nerves.

'I will leave you both to—confide together,' he murmured then, and his hand slid away from Lizzy's back.

He strode away towards the bar to greet some friends, the loose-limbed elegance with which he moved holding Lizzy's gaze though she didn't want it to.

'Lizzy, you have to tell me what's wrong with Bianca,' Sofia Moreno insisted, setting Lizzy's eyelashes flickering as she moved them away from Luc. 'She is behaving strangely and I cannot seem to get a pleasant word out of her. She should be down here by now standing with Luciano to greet their guests, but when I went to her suite after I knocked on your door she wasn't even dressed!'

'She had a headache at lunch and went to her room to rest,' Lizzy recalled with a frown. 'Perhaps she fell asleep.'

'Which would explain the rumpled bed,' Bianca's mother said tensely, 'and the way she looked like she'd just fallen out of it *and* the way she snapped off my head!'

'Give her a few more minutes to get herself together,' Lizzy suggested soothingly. 'If she still hasn't put in an appearance, I'll go up and chivvy her on.'

'In the bad mood she's in, only you dare to do it, *cara*,' Bianca's mother said tautly.

Not Bianca's betrothed? Lizzy wondered dryly as she linked her arm through Mrs Moreno's and led her back to where the rest of the guests were gathered. A few seconds later she was being warmly greeted by Bianca's father, Giorgio, and introduced to a cousin of Bianca's she hadn't met before.

Vito Moreno was about her own age and blessed with the Moreno dark good looks and a pair of laughing blue eyes. 'So you're Elizabeth,' he said. 'I've been hearing a lot about you since I arrived here this afternoon.'

'Who from?' Lizzy demanded.

'My dear cousin, of course.' Vito grinned. 'Bianca insists you are the one person who saved her from a life of rebellion and wickedness when she had to leave Sydney to live in the UK and attend the "stuffiest school around".'

Ah. 'You're one of the Sydney Morenos,' Lizzy realised. 'I recognise the accent now.'

'I used to be Bianca's partner in crime before you took my place,' he explained.

'You're *that* cousin?' She laughed up at him. 'I've heard all about you too.'

'That's my pulling power shot to death.' Vito sighed.

A long fluted glass of fizzing champagne appeared in front of Lizzy and she glanced up as she accepted it to find Luc standing over her like some dark towering giant.

'Oh—thank you,' she murmured.

He just nodded his dark head, sent an acknowledging nod towards Vito and drifted away again leaving Lizzy feeling—odd.

Then Vito said something and with a mental shrug she pushed Luc De Santis to one side and wished to goodness he would stay there for good. The minutes wore on, the mezzanine bar slowly filled with guests and still there was no sign of Bianca. Eventually people began to get restless, checking the time on their watches.

Lizzy's gaze drifted towards Luc De Santis. He was standing apart from everyone else talking into his cell phone—and was not very happy by the stern look on his face.

Was he talking to Bianca? She would not be surprised because she'd seen him angered before by Bianca's habit of always being late.

Well, get used to it, she told him silently as she watched him snap shut his mobile and slide it into his jacket pocket. Bianca's blithe lack of awareness to time and space was the constant bane of her mother's and Lizzy's lives. He could count himself lucky if she managed to turn up on time at the church next week.

As the minutes dragged on, though, even Lizzy found she had to fight the need to keep checking her watch, and Sofia Moreno was sending her pleading looks. She was about to excuse herself to go and find out what Bianca was doing when there was a sudden stir by the lifts.

Everyone turned to look as one. The following silence held like a shaken heartbeat because there, at last, was Bianca, looking an absolute vision dressed in billowing gold silk. Her long dark hair was up in a dramatically simple style that showed off the sweet perfection of her face and the slender length of her creamy smooth neck. Diamonds sparkled at her ears and her throat.

Thread a tiara into her hair and she could be a princess, Lizzy thought fondly as eyes like huge pools of liquid dark chocolate scanned her audience, then her soft mouth took on an apologetic tilt.

'Sorry I'm so late, everyone,' Bianca chanted quietly, and the mezzanine bar stirred to the sound of a beautifully directed indulgent response.

'That's my brave girl,' Lizzy thought she heard Vito murmur beneath his breath and she glanced at him sharply, but saw nothing in his expression to warrant such a strange remark.

Then Luc was striding forward to take hold of Bianca's slender fingers and lifting them to his lips. Whatever he said to his betrothed brought a sheen to Bianca's eyes and a vulnerable tremor to her oh, so beautiful mouth.

He loves her, Lizzy realised in that moment. An odd little sensation clutched at her chest. Frowning slightly, she turned away from the two lovers and was relieved to feel the sensation fade.

They were ferried to the opera in a fleet of sleek limousines. Vito Moreno was obviously meant to partner her tonight and he made her laugh, which made her relax more and more as the evening wore on. La Scala was fabulous, an experience Lizzy really enjoyed—mainly because she'd successfully managed to avoid being placed anywhere near her best friend's disturbing fiancé. Afterwards they moved on to have dinner in a beautiful sixteenth century palazzo on the outskirts of Milan.

It was all very stylish, very much a glimpse of how the richer half lived. There was dancing as well as dining, and because Vito kept on filling her wineglass Lizzy was tipsy by the time Luc De Santis arrived by her chair to invite her to dance.

There was a hovering second while she hunted around for an excuse to refuse him, then his hand arrived beneath her elbow to propel her to her feet. 'Come on,' he said dryly. 'It is expected that the groom dances at least once with his bride's maid of honour.'

Lizzy thought that was supposed to happen after the wedding, but the telling quiver struck again making her too tense and too breathless to say it as he drew her against him on the dance floor and smoothly urged her to dance.

The lights were low, the music a slow romantic ballad accompanied by a female singer with a stirringly deep and sensual voice. She felt her heart begin to pump to a heavier beat as they moved together and she absorbed the full disturbing impact of his masculine warmth and his muscular hardness pressing against her tense, softer shape.

'Relax,' he prompted after a few seconds. 'This is supposed to be an enjoyable pastime.'

Lizzy looked up, caught the mocking glow in his eyes and felt the sting of heat flush her cheeks. 'I'm just not used to—'

'Being held this close to a man?' he mocked.

'Dancing in these shoes!' she corrected hotly. 'And that wasn't a very nice thing to say.'

He just laughed, the sound low and deep and disturbingly intimate the way it resonated against the tips of her breasts. 'You are an unusual creature, Elizabeth Hadley,' he informed her then. 'You are very beautiful but you don't like to be told so. You are tense and defensive around me yet you can completely relax with a serial womaniser like Vito Moreno.'

'Vito isn't a womaniser,' Lizzy rejected. 'He's too laid back to be a womaniser.'

'Ring any telephone number in Sydney and just mention his name.'

And that was cynicism, not mockery, she noted. 'Well, I like him,' she stated stubbornly.

'Ah, I see he is beginning to reel you in.'

'And that wasn't very nice, either!'

His dark head suddenly dipped, bringing his lips very close to her cheek. 'I'll let you into a secret, *mia bella*—I am not very nice.'

He was so close now she could smell the masculine pull of his tangy scent. Lizzy jerked her head back. 'Well, you had better be nice to Bianca,' she warned loyally.

He just laughed as he straightened up again, then drew her even closer so he could control her movements with a cool, casual strength. He was taller than her by several impacting inches, which put her eyes on a level with his strong, chiselled chin. They didn't speak again, and as the dance wore on maybe it was the fault of too many recklessly consumed glasses of wine that made her so aware of everything about him. Even the smooth feel of his silk lapel beneath her fingers fascinated her, and the bright whiteness of his shirt against the natural olive tones of his throat.

He was gorgeous. There was just no use in trying to deny it. Everything about him was so perfectly presented from the neatly styled gloss of his satin black hair to the length of his very Italian nose and the truly beautiful shape to his mouth.

And the singer droned on, low and soulful. Lizzy felt the sensual pull of the melody percolate her system as potently as the wine she had been drinking all evening and like a fool she closed her eyes and just let the sensation carry her away. One set of his long golden fingers lightly clasped her pale slender fingers, the other set rested low in the arch of her back. She had no idea how her fingers were stroking the silk lapel of his jacket or that she had moved in so close to him that her breath was softly feathering his throat. She just moved where he guided her, aware of the tingling tension affecting her body but unaware that it was affecting him too. His fingers moved slightly against her clasped fingers, the hand at her back glided upwards to the centre of her spine and gently urged her into even closer contact with him.

It was—nice. Kind of tingly and floaty and she hadn't a clue as to how much she had relaxed into him until she felt the living warmth of taut skin brush against her lips and tasted it on the tip of her tongue.

With a jerk of shock Lizzy flicked her eyes open and pulled back her head. Dismay instantly curled its way through her body accompanied by a wave of mortified embarrassment that flooded like fire into her face when she realised what she had done.

She had just brushed her lips against Bianca's fiancé's throat and tasted him with her tongue!

CHAPTER TWO

'OH, MY GOD,' Lizzy gasped in skin quivering consternation.

They weren't even dancing any longer! And he was looking down at her with one of those dreadful mocking smiles tugging at the corners of his mouth!

Dropping her eyes to his throat, Lizzy wished with all her pounding heart that the ground would just open up and swallow her whole.

'I'm so sorry!' she whispered, stepping back from him so violently she almost went over on the spindly heels of her shoes.

'In truth I was rather flattered by the—compliment.' His hand snaked out to steady her. 'Fortunately I sensed it coming, which is why we are now standing outside on the terrace away from curious eyes…'

Outside—? Glancing dizzily around her, sure enough, Lizzy discovered that they were indeed standing on a shadowy terrace she had not even known was here! Realisation hit as to how engrossed she must have been in him that he'd been able to manoeuvre her through a pair of open French windows out into the cooler evening air without her even being aware!

Once again she took a shaky step backwards—right out of his reach this time—and thankfully managed to remain safely upright. The music still droned somewhere in the near distance. Mortification riddled her blood. She wanted to die and she couldn't look at him—didn't know what to say in her own defence!

And he was so relaxed, his hips resting against a heavy stone balustrade, his arms lightly folded across his wide chest, and she had the sickly feeling he was thoroughly—thoroughly enjoying himself.

'Blame the wine,' he offered gently.

Lizzy nodded, pathetically grateful for the miserable excuse. 'I'm not used to drinking so m-much.'

'No,' he agreed.

'And Vito—'

'Was constantly filling up your glass.'

She hadn't been going to say that, but hearing him say it brought her eyes flickering up to his face. 'He wasn't!' she protested, then swallowed and added helplessly, 'W-was he?'

'Poor Elizabeth,' the cool brute murmured. 'Caught by the oldest trick in the book.'

Then she remembered what she had been doing with him and she dragged her eyes away from him to wave a decidedly uncoordinated hand towards the French doors.

'I th-think I should…'

'Go back inside to him so he can intoxicate you some more?'

'No.' The waving fingers tightened into a fist and dropped to her side. 'You have a very nasty sense of humour, *signor*.'

'And you, *signorina*, have a very moist tongue and a warm, soft pair of lips.'

That was it, Lizzy couldn't take any more of this, he'd had

enough fun at her expense. Spinning on her heel, she turned towards the doors.

'What are the two of you doing alone out here?' a new voice suddenly intruded.

And nothing, nothing in all of her twenty-two years, had ever made Lizzy feel as bad as she felt then when her friend—her beautiful, happily in love *loyal* best friend—stepped through those same French doors.

'Your—maid of honour was feeling the heat,' Luc responded evenly. 'She needed to breathe some fresh air.'

Barely holding herself together, Lizzy felt her insides squirm with guilt and shame when Bianca looked at her and said, 'Are you okay, sweetie?' with genuine concern. '*Dio*, you do looked flushed, Lizzy.'

'Blame your cousin,' Luc suggested. 'He is the one who's been topping up her wineglass all evening.'

'Vito? Oh, the wicked boy. And I told him to take care of you for me…' She floated across the terrace to place a comforting arm across Lizzy's shoulders. 'With your sternly temperate papa you're just not used to late nights and partying are you, *cara*? In fact you are *not* used to drinking alcohol at all!'

'My father isn't that bad,' Lizzy mumbled, feeling more uncomfortable by the second.

'No, he's worse,' Bianca said curtly, doing nothing to hide her dislike of Lizzy's father, the man she still blamed for breaking up her love affair with Matthew two years ago. 'I'm still surprised that he actually allowed you to come here knowing you would have to enjoy yourself! I even had to provide you with clothes so you were not forced to turn out in those terrible modest sacks he prefers you to wear!'

Wanting to curl up inside her own skin now at this small piece of insensitivity, Lizzy wondered helplessly if this was punishment for what she'd been doing with Bianca's man.

Surprisingly it was Luc De Santis who came to her defence, 'That's enough, *cara*,' he said to Bianca. 'Modesty is not a sin. And your friend has a—headache,' he offered up. 'Hearing you chatter on about things she would rather not discuss in front of me is making it worse.'

'Oh, sorry, Lizzy. I'm such a mean mouthed thing,' Bianca said contritely. 'Tell you what, why don't I take you back to the hotel? We could both do with an early night and Luc won't mind, will you, *caro*?'

This could only get worse if a rat jumped over the balustrade and told Bianca the full gruesome truth about why her best friend was out here with her man, Lizzy thought as she suffered Bianca's contrition with a lump in her throat that was threatening to turn into tears.

'Of course not,' the smooth-voiced man himself agreed.

'N-no—really.' She was almost consumed by self-hate, 'I can't let you leave your own party. Vito said he was going soon to catch up on his jet lag. I'll—I'll go back to the hotel with him.'

'No, I won't hear of it,' her wretched best friend said firmly. 'And Vito can come back with us so I can tell him off for getting you sloshed. Luc will organise a car.'

Dutifully, Luc De Santis straightened out of his relaxed pose against the balustrade. Lizzy cringed inside and refused to look at him as he strode past them to go inside.

She should confess, she *needed* to confess—but how could she? Bianca would be shocked. She might never forgive her. Their friendship would be over for good.

But what if Luc told her first? What if he thought it would make an amusing story to relay to his betrothed? How was she ever going to live with it if he did?

They were about to step into the limo when Luc touched Lizzy's arm. 'Don't do it, she will never forgive you,' he warned so softly that only she could hear him, shocking her further that he could read her mind. 'And if you have any sense you will steer clear of Vito Moreno,' he added grimly.

Then he turned to his fiancée to offer her a brief kiss good-night.

Vito's company in the car made the journey a whole lot easier for Lizzy because she could pretend to doze while he and Bianca talked. It vaguely occurred to her that the conversation was hushed and heated, but she assumed Bianca was keeping her promise to give him a hard time for the trick with the wine so she didn't listen.

And anyway, she did have a headache, one of those dull, throbbing aches that came when you didn't like yourself and knew the feeling was not going to change any time soon. When the two cousins decided to have a last drink in the bar before they went to their rooms, Lizzy made her escape and spent the night with her head stuffed beneath her pillow, trying not to remember what she had done.

But she should have listened to what the other two had been saying, she discovered early the next morning when hell arrived with the sound of urgent knocking on her door. If she'd listened she might have been able to stop Bianca from making the biggest mistake of her life.

As it was, all she could do was stand and listen in growing horror while Sofia Moreno poured it all out between thick, shaking sobs.

'She's gone!' Bianca's *mamma* choked out hysterically the moment that Lizzy open her door. 'She just packed all her things in the middle of the night and left the hotel! All this time and she never showed a single sign that they were planning this between them! How could she? How could he? What are people going to say? What about Luciano? Oh, I don't think I can bear it. She has thrown away a wonderful future. How could she do this to us? How could your foolish brother just turn up here and steal her away?'

Having assumed that Mrs Moreno had been referring to Vito, *'Matthew?'* Lizzy choked out in disbelief. 'Are you sure you meant my brother, Mrs Moreno?' she prompted unsteadily.

'Of course I mean Matthew!' the older woman shook out. 'He arrived here yesterday afternoon, apparently. He was *hiding* in Bianca's bathroom when I went to see her yesterday! Can you imagine it? She wasn't dressed and the bed was rumpled! *Dio mio*, it does not take much to guess what had been going on! Did you know about what they were planning to do, Elizabeth—did you?'

The fierce accusation straightened Lizzy's backbone. *'No,'* she denied adamantly. 'I'm as shocked about this as you are!'

'Well, I hope that is true,' Mrs Moreno said coldly. 'For I will never forgive you if you played along with this inexcusable thing!'

'I thought you meant she'd gone away with Vito,' Lizzy murmured dazedly.

'Vito? He's her cousin! Are you trying to make this situation worse than it already is?'

Thoroughly chastened by the appalled response, Lizzy could only mumble out an apology.

'Now someone is going to have to break the news to Luciano,' Bianca's mother sobbed. 'Bianca has left him a note but Luciano went to his Lake Como villa last night to prepare for our arrival tomorrow and my husband has left for the city to see to some business this morning—he doesn't even know yet what his wicked daughter has done to ruin our lives!'

The Villa De Santis stood on top of a rocky outcrop, its pale lemon walls kissed by the softening light of the afternoon sun.

Lizzy's stomach gave a nauseous flutter as she stepped from the water taxi onto the villa's private jetty with its newly painted ribs standing out in the brilliant sunshine against the darkness of the older wood. Another boat was already moored there, a sleek, racy-looking thing that completely demoralised the water taxi as it nudged in beside it.

Bianca's father had arranged for a car to bring her as far as Bellagio. They'd discussed if they should ring Luc to break the news to him, then decided he should be told face to face. At first Giorgio Moreno was going to make the trip himself, but he'd looked so ill that Lizzy had offered to come in his place.

His heart wasn't good and she felt responsible. How could she not feel responsible when it was her brother who'd caused all of this? But after her own utter stupidity of the night before the last thing she wanted to do right now was to come face to face with Luc De Santis.

The old quiver struck as she walked towards the iron gates that she assumed would lead to steps up to the villa. Behind her, she could hear the water taxi already moving away, its engines growling as it churned up the glinting blue water, leaving her feeling as if she had just been marooned on the worst place on earth.

A man appeared from out of the shadows on the other side of the gate, stopping her in her tracks with his piercing dark eyes that looked her up and down. She had to look a mess because she certainly felt one with her hair hanging loose round her pale face. And she was still wearing the same green top and white capris she'd pulled on so hurriedly this morning when Bianca's *mamma* had knocked on her door.

'May I help you, *signorina*?' the man questioned in coolly polite Italian.

Passing her nervous tongue across her lips, 'I've come with a letter for Signor De Santis,' Lizzy explained. 'M-my name is Elizabeth Hadley.'

He nodded his head and produced a cell phone, his dark eyes not leaving her for a second while he spoke quietly to whoever was listening on the other end. Then with another nod he unlocked the gate and opened it. 'You can go up, *signorina*,' he sanctioned.

With a murmured thanks Lizzy was about to step past him when a sudden thought made her stop. 'I-I will need a water taxi back to Bellagio,' she told him. 'I didn't think to ask the other one to wait.'

'I will see to it when you are ready to leave,' he assured her.

Offering another husky 'thank you', Lizzy continued on her way to discover a set of age-worn stone steps cut into the rock face. At the top of the steps she found soft green lawns and carefully tended gardens and a path leading to a stone terrace beyond which stood the villa with its long windows thrown open to the softest of breezes coming off the lake.

Beautiful, she thought, but that was as far as her observations went. She was too uptight, too anxious—scared witless, if she was going to be honest.

Another man was waiting for her on the terrace. He offered her a small stately bow and invited her to follow him. It was cool inside the villa, the decoration a mix of warm colours hung with beautiful tapestries and paintings in ornate gold frames. The man led the way to a pair of heavy wood doors, knocked, then opened one of them before stepping to one side in a silent invitation for her to pass through.

Needing to take in a deep breath before she could make herself go any further, Lizzy walked past the servant into a beautiful room with high stucco ceilings and long narrow windows that flooded the room with soft golden light. The walls were pale, the furniture dark and solid like the richly polished floor beneath her feet. Shelves lined with books filled narrow alcoves; a heavy stone fireplace dominated one wall. As she spun her gaze over sumptuously ancient dark red velvet chairs and elegant sofas she finally settled on the huge heavily carved desk set between two of the windows—and the man who was standing tall and still behind it.

Tension instantly grabbed hold of her throat and sent her heart sinking to her toes. He already knew about Bianca, Lizzy realised. It was stamped right there on his grimly cold face.

'You have a letter for me, I believe,' Luc De Santis prompted. No greeting, no attempt whatsoever to make this easier for her.

But then why should he—? 'H-how did you know?' Lizzy dared to ask him.

His eyes made a brief flick down her front, then away again. 'She was to be my wife. The position made her vulnerable to a certain kind of low-life out on the make, so of course I had a security team watching her.'

But they didn't stop her running away with Matthew? Lizzy would have loved to have asked the question but the way he was standing there in a steel-dark razor-sharp business suit and with his face carved into such cold, hard angles, the question remained just a thick lump in her throat as she made herself walk forward, feeling as if she were stepping on sharp needles all the way.

Coming to a halt in front of the desk, she set down the letter. Her heart was pounding in her ears as he held her still with his gaze for a taut second or two before he reached out and picked the letter up, then let yet another few seconds stretch before he finally broke the envelope seal.

After that there was nothing, just a long, long numbing silence while he stood behind his desk reading the words Bianca had used to jilt him with, and Lizzy stood with her eyes fixed helplessly on his lean dark face, aware that the power of his innate pride had to be the only thing stopping him from diminishing to a used and broken man.

'I'm—sorry,' she mumbled, knowing it was a wincingly inadequate thing to say but—what else was there for her to say?

He gave a curt nod of his head, eyes like gold crystal set between heavy black eyelashes still fixed on the single sheet of paper even as he slowly set it down on the desk.

'You were offered no forewarning of this?'

Lizzy felt her nails bite into the tender skin of her palms as she closed them into tense, anxious fists. 'Nothing,' she answered.

'Her family?'

She gave a helpless shake of her head. 'Y-you were there last night—she looked radiant. She—'

'My future bride basking in the glory of her good fortune,' he drawled in a cold, mocking lilt.

Pressing her lips together, Lizzy lowered her gaze and said nothing. It was so obvious now that Bianca had been putting on a fabulous act aimed to fool all of them last night. Now it all felt so horrible, the extravagantly romantic glitter and gloss just a huge cruel con. She'd floated around like a princess in her gold silk. She'd clung to this man, smiled at him so starry-eyed and in love. And everyone had smiled as they'd watched her, everyone had remarked on what a fabulous couple they made. Even Luc with his rather sardonic way of looking at everything had smiled for his beautiful be-trothed. In some dark corner of her being, Lizzy had been dreadfully envious because not many women got to live their childhood dream of falling in love with and marrying her prince.

Not that Luc De Santis was a prince, because he wasn't. He was just formed from the same mould handsome princes came out of, with his tall dark good looks and his perfectly constructed body and the added kudos of inherited vast wealth that had come to him down through centuries of careful De Santis bridal selection.

Dynasties, Bianca had called it. 'I'm marrying into a dynasty because I have the right name and the right genetic fingerprint.'

It had been such a cynical thing to say that Lizzy had been shocked. 'But you love him, don't you?'

'Are you joking, *cara*?' she'd laughed. 'You've seen him. What girl in her right mind wouldn't fall in love with Luc? Even you if you were given the chance.'

Lizzy's slender shoulders twitched in guilty response to

the sound of that airy challenge ringing inside her head, because she knew she had already developed a kind of fascination for this man and it nagged her conscience to death—especially after last night. But she also frowned because it was only now as she stood here having to face the fallout from her best friend's stunning deception that it was occurring to her just how cleverly Bianca had skirted around the question of her loving this man.

She watched as Luc picked up the letter again, long brown fingers lifting up the single sheet of snowy white of paper to re-read yet again what Bianca had written to him. His face remained cold—completely expressionless—yet Lizzy discovered that she couldn't breathe. It had something to do with the way his lips were being held in such a steady flat line and the way his nostrils flared as he drew in a breath.

He was angry, she realised, and she didn't blame him. Whether his heart was devastated was difficult to tell. The few occasions she'd been in his company—even last night—he'd always struck her as someone who did not feel much of anything.

Cold, hard, unemotional, arrogant, she found herself listing as she stood here waiting for him to speak. She supposed she could tag on other words like tall, dark and disgustingly gorgeous but all those words did was to describe his potently masculine outer shell. It was the first description that really said it all about the inner man.

The long silence dragged until it picked at her nerve-ends. In one part of her consciousness Lizzy knew she should be getting out of here now that she'd delivered the letter, but she was oddly reluctant to leave him alone.

She still felt responsible—though her common sense told

her she wasn't. She felt—pity for him, though she knew he would probably be utterly contemptuous of her for daring to feel it.

Strange man, she thought, not for the first time, as she stood on the other side of the desk unable to take her eyes off his face. For all of his wealth and his power and high standing in Italian society she had never seen him as anything other than a man who stood alone. Even when he'd been with Bianca she'd sensed a reserve in him she had never been able to adequately explain.

'I…I suppose you're wondering where your engagement ring is,' she blurted out, needing to say something to fill in the unbearably tense empty space, and the ring had come up in discussion when Bianca's mother had said the same thing.

'No,' he denied without any inflection whatsoever. 'I would imagine that running off with a poor man has already sealed the ring's fate.'

Lizzy winced, cheeks heating at this cool reminder of the other issue in all of this she was having to deal with—the fact that the man Bianca had run off with also happened to be her very own brother.

'Matt isn't poor.' She felt compelled to defend Matthew's middle class earnings. It was, after all, the only thing about him she felt she could defend right now.

'In your estimation or mine?'

Oh, that was so very arrogant of him. Lizzy felt anger begin to rise even though she knew she didn't have the right to let it. 'Look—' with a tense twist she turned to the door '—I think I had better leave you to—'

'Running away like the other two?' he mocked her.

'No,' she denied that. 'I just think it's better that I go before I lose my temper.'

'So you have one?'

'Yes.' She swung back round only to find that he had come around the desk so quickly and silently she hadn't heard him move. Now he was leaning against it with his arms folded across his chest, Bianca's letter lying discarded on the desk behind him.

Surprise brought a soft gasp whispering from her throat. And a new kind of tension flared in the pit of her stomach at the way he was studying the little green top and white capris she'd pulled on so hurriedly this morning, and the wildly unruly state of her hair.

Last night she'd made a fool of herself with him. This morning she'd been awoken by hysterics and accusations from Bianca's parents that still rang in her head. Now this— this deeply unsettling man she'd been sent to face because Bianca's parents couldn't bring themselves to do it—and he was looking her over as if he couldn't believe she would dare to walk out of her room looking as she did.

Well, you try applying make-up when your fingers won't stop shaking, she told him silently as she suffered his cool appraisal that was so spiked by the glint of contempt. You try wondering what clothes to wear for an audience with a jilted man when your nerves were shot to death at the very prospect.

'During the week you have been here in my country I've watched you play the straight man to Bianca's high-strung and volatile temperament,' he said so suddenly it made Lizzy blink. 'I've watched you soothe her, calm her and even humour her. But I do not recall seeing you threaten to lose your temper with her even when she took it upon herself to mock or embarrass you, so why do you feel the need to lose your temper with me?'

'Y-you attacked my family.'

'I *attacked* your brother,' he amended. 'You don't believe I have the right?'

Of course he had the right. This time yesterday he had been one half of a glittering couple, his marriage to Bianca only a short week away. It was supposed to be the wedding of the year here in Italy, now it was about to become juicy fodder for every media outlet and it was her very own brother who'd turned it into that.

Lizzy moved jerkily, offering a small conciliatory flip of one hand despite feeling as though she were being whipped by his smooth cutting tone. 'I give you the right to despise my brother,' she acknowledged. 'I will even give you the right to be angry with me because I'm the sister of the man who ran off with your bride. But I will not—' and her chin came up, eyes sparking with challenge '—stand here and let you deride the fact that we are not rich like you.'

'I did that?'

Lizzy pressed her lips together and nodded. He wasn't the only one around her who'd had his pride battered today. She'd had to put up with some pretty mean observations from Bianca's parents about her brother that had been difficult to swallow down.

'Then I apologise.'

Lizzy didn't believe him. Facing up to him like this, she didn't see or hear so much as a hint of apology in his tone. But, 'Thank you,' she responded politely anyway. 'Now if you don't mind, I'll leave you to—'

'How did you get here?'

Once again she was about to turn away when he stopped her. 'By water taxi across the lake from Bellagio,' she said.

He nodded. 'Then it seems to me that you're stuck here until I arrange your return across the lake.'

'Y-your man on the jetty said he would see to—'

'It's a case of priorities, Miss Hadley,' he cut in. 'My instructions take precedence around here, you see.'

He was pulling rank, Lizzy recognised, lips parting to say something then snapping shut again when it suddenly struck her that he was burning for a fight.

Did she take him on? The question lit up her brain while her common sense told her to just get the heck out of here because she wasn't up to his weight. He lived in this fabulous villa on the banks of Lake Como, he owned a beautiful apartment in Milan, which was why she'd been so surprised to find he'd taken a suite at the hotel last night, and at least three more fabulous homes Bianca had mentioned set in different parts of the world. He lived the high-powered jet setting lifestyle of the world's business heavyweights. He even flew the world in comfort in his very own executive jet.

And just out there tied to his private jetty floated his sleek glinting white private power boat that could spin her back across the lake in ten minutes—but he was refusing to give the order because he felt the need to kick someone around a bit and she happened to be conveniently there.

Lizzy looked away from him then back again, not at all sure what to do next. 'You do know you're being petty,' she sighed out finally.

'Green,' he murmured.

'Green—what?' she flicked out, completely thrown by the comment.

'Your eyes when you're angry,' he provided. 'Most of the time they are a soft placid grey.'

'They can spit pretty sharp daggers too when I'm cornered,' she reacted.

'Let me test that,' he offered. 'You have known all along what they were planning.'

It was not a question. 'No,' Lizzy insisted. 'I *told* you I did not know.'

But even as she said it her insides were creasing guiltily because perhaps she had seen it coming only it had been so much simpler to just block it out.

'I did not have you down as a liar, Elizabeth,' he said coolly.

'I'm not lying!' Frowning—annoyed with herself as well as with him *and* this horrible position she'd been put in, 'I did not see it coming,' she insisted a second time, 'but I admit I feel some responsibility because I think I should have done.'

'Because you knew they were lovers?'

Did he have to put it as calmly as that? Shifting her tense stance, 'Yes,' she answered, deciding to be blunt with him since he didn't seem to possess a single sensitive nerve in his body. 'For a while, several years ago.'

'Childhood sweethearts.' His hard mouth flicked out the semblance of a smile.

A bit more than that, she thought as she pinned her lips together and made no comment at all. Then, because she couldn't take the probing glint in his eyes, she let out a sigh. 'You were right about the wealth difference meaning something. He's never going to be good enough for her you know.'

'Whereas I hit all the right criteria for a Moreno?'

Lizzy offered a shrug this time—what else could she do?

He did hit all the right criteria. He was everything the Morenos expected their beautiful daughter to marry. Matthew wasn't. Matthew came right out of middle class England. He'd enjoyed the necessary public-school education to give him a great kick-start in life but that was about it. Until this recent financial crisis her family had survived comfortably on its small business income—no more, no less. Matthew was expected to take over the business from their father one day and to marry some nice middle class Englishwoman who would not demand more from him than he was able to provide.

Bianca on the other hand was always going to expect more. She was always going to have what she wanted in life even if it meant providing it herself. Matthew wouldn't be able to cope with that. His ego would take such a hard knocking he'd never be happy, whereas this man had so much money of his own he wouldn't give a toss as to how his beautiful wife spent her own money, and *his* ego would stay firmly intact.

'She will come back,' she promised. 'She just needs time to—sort her head out.'

'Not her heart?' The dry distinction made Lizzy wince.

'I'm sure she loves you,' she persisted. 'She's just not ready to commit to marriage. If you just give her time, then I—'

Black eyebrows with a fascinating silken gloss arched her a curious look. 'Are you actually standing there, Miss Hadley, suggesting that I should wait for Bianca to sort her head out?'

Well, was she? Lifting her chin, 'If you love her—yes,' she insisted.

'Then you are a romantic fool because it is not going to happen.' He moved suddenly, straightening away from the desk. 'There is a wedding arranged for next Saturday morning and I intend to make sure that it goes ahead.'

Without a bride? Lizzy stared at him. 'You mean—you're going to find her and drag her back to marry you?' A silly kind of laugh left her throat at the very image of Bianca being dragged by this man down the church aisle kicking and screaming.

'No.' Reaching behind him, his long fingers picked Bianca's letter up again—this time to fold it with slow, neat precision. 'I mean to replace her with someone else.'

She was pretty much held in his thrall by now. 'Just like that?'

'Just like that.' He nodded and made her gasp as he ripped the letter into small pieces, then calmly dropped them into the waste-paper basket standing by the desk.

It was such a cold act of dismissal of Bianca and everything she should mean to him that Lizzy began to feel slightly sick.

'You will have to move quickly to put your life in order, of course, but with my assistance I think it can be achieved in time.'

She dragged her eyes up from the discarded pieces of paper. It took a few seconds for his words to actually sink in— then they did sink in and Lizzy took a jerky step backwards.

'M-my life is fine as it is.'

'I don't doubt it,' he acknowledged. 'But will it be *fine* by tomorrow when I inform the authorities that your brother has emptied your company bank account?'

CHAPTER THREE

'Th-That was not in the least bit funny,' Lizzy husked out, her heart beginning to thump heavily against her ribs because this conversation had just taken a sinister turn for the bad. 'I know you're hurt and angry, and I accept you feel the need to kick someone around in response. But that doesn't give you the right to lie about my family!'

'Your *brother*.' Once again Luc made the distinction. 'I restrict my accusations to only one member of your family. The rest I will honour with the benefit of the doubt—for now.'

He was losing her with every cool word he threw at her. 'You suspect my *father* of being a crook? Where do you get off believing you can say something like that?'

'I "get off", as you so nicely describe it, by being a banker,' he responded. 'And being a banker I am not prone to let my heart rule my head.'

'You've lost me.' Lizzy stared at him in bewilderment.

'Then let me explain. Bianca is a very wealthy woman.'

'I know that,' she snapped out.

'A little—shall we call it family ingenuity?—and she could be misled into believing that her childhood sweetheart had hit it rich.'

'I think you need time on your own for some quiet con-
templation,' Lizzy told him curtly, and did what she should
have done minutes before and turned on her heel to leave.

'Your—close relationship to her made me curious,' he
continued smoothly as she walked. 'So I decided it would be
wise to have you and your family checked out.'

'Checked out?' Once again she swung round to stare at
him. 'So where the heck do you get off *now* thinking you have
the right to do that?'

'The right of Bianca's future husband who was—er—
puzzled by your close friendship to her. You're not her type,
Miss Hadley,' he stated bluntly. 'Anyone with eyes can see
that Bianca comes from a different side of the fence, yet here
you are, staying in the best hotel in Milan paid for with her
family's money, wearing clothes she has bought for you so
you would not look out of place in the company of her rich
friends, and about to play the honoured role at her wedding
as her chief bridesmaid.'

'*Was* about to,' she hit back, infuriated by the nasty slant
he was putting on everything.

'Was,' he acknowledged with a cool dip of his dark head.
'So I decided to do some checking, and guess what I found
out? Hadley's is not merely enjoying a temporary cash crisis
as I was given to believe, it is about to go under altogether.
Your father is in debt up to his neck. Your brother hates the
whole engineering scenario and resents the fact that he is
expected to stay in the business.'

Lizzy flushed. 'Matthew wanted to be an artist.'

'Oh, how romantically right for him,' her persecutor
mocked. 'With his golden good looks and his ravaged sen-
sibilities he makes the perfect rescue for an impressionable

thing like Bianca—whereas you,' he went on before Lizzy could say anything, 'you make the perfect level-headed foil to keep Bianca's starry eyes blinded to what your brother is really about.'

Lizzy straightened her trembling tense shoulders. 'Have you quite finished slaughtering my family?' she demanded, wanting to slap his face.

'Haughty,' he remarked. 'I like it.'

'Well, I don't like you!' she hit back. 'Bianca and I have been friends since we were twelve years old—her wealth or my lack of it has never been an issue between us because that's not what true friendship is about! *My* family works hard for its living, *signor*,' she defended proudly. '*All* of us work hard! *My* father did not waste his life swanning around the world enjoying the useless life of an overindulged playboy from a filthy rich but totally dysfunctional family from which you, sadly, were the cynical end result! And *if* my brother is different from the rest of us at least he knows he is loved! Whereas you, *signor*, with your untold wealth and your inherited arrogance, can't ever have been loved to be so cold and suspicious of everything and everyone that you have to dig into their lives behind their backs!'

'Dysfunctional?' His glinting gold eyes narrowed on her. 'You have a very cynical view of *my* family history, Miss Hadley. It makes me curious as to where you collected *your* information and, more interestingly, why you did.'

Lizzy tensed as if he'd shot her. She'd walked herself right into that prickly trap. 'I…Bianca,' she said, hating the hot rush of colour that mounted her cheeks because she knew she'd been guilty of spending hours looking him up on the internet. 'She described marrying you as joining a dynasty because she had the right name and the right genetic finger-print,' she crashed on. 'It sounded so cold and businesslike to me that I thought she was joking at the time, but now I see that she wasn't joking at all or you would be standing there too overwhelmed by your broken heart to even think of putting such a cold suggestion to me!'

'Finished?' he asked when she finally ran down to a breathless choke.

Shaking all over now, Lizzy pressed her trembling lips together and nodded.

So did he, and straightened from the desk. 'Then with the character assassination over we will return to the subject of our wedding,' he said.

'I am *not* marrying you!' Lizzy all but shrieked at him. Was he mad?

He moved round the desk. 'You kissed me last night.'

The reminder forced her into dragging in a sharp intake of breath. She'd hoped he'd forgotten it. She'd prayed all night long that she'd just dreamt up that awful, shocking stolen kiss.

'I was drunk—'

'You appeared to be.' He was opening a drawer now and taking out a thick folder which he placed on the desk. 'Of course, you could have been playing with me as diversion-ary tactics to keep my eyes blinded to what Bianca was up to.'

She was so stunned by that cynical slant on her stupid be-haviour, when she opened her mouth nothing came out of it.

He smiled—coolly. 'Everything is open to misinterpreta-tion, Elizabeth. When you—came on to me like some very tipsy sweet, shy virgin, I was—flattered. Now?' He flipped open the file. 'How different things can look in the cool light of day and with common sense re-established. Come and take a look…'

It was not a suggestion. Lizzy felt a tingling prickle spread across the surface of her skin as she forced her shaky legs to move back to the desk. He twisted the file around, then stabbed at it with a long finger to draw her eyes down.

She found herself staring at a bank statement—a bank statement with the Hadley name printed at its head. 'H-how did you get hold of that?' she whispered.

'I'm a banker,' he reminded her—again. 'With the right contacts and the right strings to pull I can get anything I want.'

There was a double meaning in that remark that did not pass by Lizzy.

'Look where I'm pointing,' he prompted.

She looked, then stilled as if turned to stone.

'The date shows that your company account received a heavy injection of funds just two days ago,' he spelled out what she had already seen.

Five and a half million…Lizzy had never seen five and a half million written down in black and white before. To her it was a gasping amount.

'If you look at the next entry,' her tormentor persisted, 'you will see that the five and a half million pounds was withdrawn again on the same day.'

'No,' she breathed, refusing to believe what it was he was implying here.

Then she jerked out of her shocked stasis. 'I need to ring my father.' White as a sheet now, she turned dizzily and headed for the door.

'You will not call anyone,' that ruthlessly calm voice instructed. 'At this precise moment I have control of this situation and I mean to hold onto it. Bringing someone else into it will risk that control.'

'Control over what?' Lizzy swung around to stare at him.

'You,' he provided. 'Until you brought me Bianca's letter I was still puzzling as to why your *father* had successfully negotiated the loan he needed to save his company only to instantly remove all the money and put it somewhere else.'

Lizzy suddenly needed to sit down somewhere. The only chair handy was the one placed several feet away from the desk. She sank into it. Her head was swimming, the complicated puzzle of what was really going on here beyond her stunned capabilities right now.

'Your brother is the only other person besides your father authorised to access this account. Put it all together, Elizabeth,' he encouraged. 'It does not take much effort to calculate that your brother has taken the money to fund his romantic elopement with Bianca. If you did play a part in their disappearance then I hope you have taken into account that you have been left here to carry the can.'

At that precise moment Lizzy didn't care what position she was sitting here in. She was worried about her father. If—*when*—he found out what Matthew had done he was going to—

'Of course, I must also point out that if you are genuinely innocent of any role in this, then you are still about to carry the can,' that oh, so hateful voice injected, 'because *I* want reparation for being taken for an idiot, and if that means putting you into Bianca's wedding dress and marrying you in her place, then that is what is going to happen.'

'For goodness' sake!' She jumped to her feet. 'Don't you

think this situation is bad enough without you trying to fly to the moon?'

He *laughed*! Lizzy couldn't believe she was hearing it! 'You have a quaint way of expressing yourself.'

If the desk hadn't been between them she would have thrown herself at him in fury! 'I am *not* marrying you!' she had to make do with shouting out.

'Why not?' Throwing himself into the chair behind the desk, he arched her a challenging look. 'Is there something wrong with me?'

'Don't ask me to make a list,' Lizzy muttered, wrapping her arms around her body and glaring at him while her mind shot off in all directions trying to find the sense in this mad situation. 'You've got the eyes of a lion,' she then heard herself murmur out of absolutely nowhere!

'Lions mark their territory, jealously protect their women, but they do not hunt,' he responded lazily.

'Is that supposed to mean something?' Lizzy snapped, wishing she'd kept her silly mouth shut about his eyes.

He offered a shrug. 'I am ready to mate. I want—cubs. I did not have to hunt for Bianca because she's always been there in the background of my life ready to claim once she'd grown up. Now here you are.' Those damned golden eyes fixed on her face. 'You don't need hunting either because I have you caught and shackled by your brother's stealing tendencies and an attraction for me you find impossible to hide.'

'I am not attracted to you in any way, shape or form,' she denied stiffly.

'Then why the sweet, tender kiss?'

'Oh, for goodness' sake.' He was like a dog with a particularly juicy bone to gnaw on. 'It wasn't a kiss! I accidentally brushed my mouth against your throat! *And* I was drunk!' she added for good measure.

'Tipsy on months of guilty lusting,' he taunted. 'Your attraction for me has been right there in your body language from the first time we met in London and you couldn't stop yourself from hungrily drinking me in,' he declared arrogantly. 'It was there when we met in the lift in Milan. It was definitely there last night when we danced together and I gave in to temptation and waltzed you out onto the terrace. And it was absolutely there in that dizzily irresistible brush you allowed your lips and the tender moist tip of your tongue to make against my throat.'

Feeling as if she were drowning in the hot steam of her own embarrassment, Lizzy struck back. 'You are more than ten years older than me, and that makes you really old in my eyes, *signor*.'

'Thirty-four to twenty-two is a good difference, *cara*.' It was the first time he had used that endearment to her and it quivered down her spine like a terrible sin. 'It means I can offer you experience and fidelity, having worked out my studding period when I was your age. Whereas you will give me your youth, your beauty, your wonderful smooth, tight, creamy white body—and your *loyalty* when you switch it from your friend and your brother to protect your father from the worst scandal you can possibly imagine if his name gets dragged into this.'

'How cold you are.' Arms tightening across her body, she shivered.

'Not between the sheets.'

'And that's it?' Lizzy flashed. 'Between the sheets I get your warmer side and your fabulous experience while out of them

I get to play the role of your very rich, very pampered, *young* trophy wife and face—saver? No affection offered, no *love*?'

'Love is an overrated fantasy.'

'Coming from you I expect that it is.'

'Are you digging at my dysfunctional family again?'

'I'm digging at the fact that I don't like you very much.'

'But you desire me like crazy,' he confided silkily.

Lizzy made a tense movement of her body, a frown like a dusky cloud settling across her face.

'You're turned on just by looking at me,' he continued relentlessly. 'You have this instinctive knowledge that the sex is going to be so good between us and it nags at you like a persistent ache. If I stepped round this desk right now and drew you into my arms you would go up like a Roman candle.'

'Without the bed and the sheets?' The sarcasm was out before she could stop it. If she'd meant it as a slap at his horrible self-confidence all it did was to make him laugh— softly, deeply, a seriously disturbing, huskily attractive sound that came from somewhere low down in his chest. 'I can be adaptable, *bella mia*, if encouraged.'

Hating his lazy, laid-back superior poise and self-assurance, she was riled into taking him on. 'So if I decided one day to, say, stroll into your office and demand sex with you while you're busy on the phone making more millions?' she challenged.

'Is that one of your fantasies?' he quizzed, bringing a flush crawling up her throat. 'Then, of course, I would do my best to accommodate you—just make sure you arrive wearing no tights.' He ran his eyes down over her. 'Panties can be dealt with, tights demand a distinct lack of finesse, and if your fantasy forces me to make millions while I accommodate you then, the easier you make it for me, the more pleasure you will get out of it.'

'God, you're insufferable.' Lizzy spun her back to him, barely able to believe the calm insolence with which he'd said all of that and despising herself for giving him the chance.

'Just more experienced at this game than you are,' he told her. 'Though sex across my desk while I talk on the telephone is novel,' he admitted. 'Maybe we will try it.'

Her slender shoulders hunched and she lifted up her hands to grab at them as if doing so would keep his outrageous suggestion out. It didn't matter that she knew she had started it. He was right and he was so much more experienced at this game so all she'd managed to do by taking him on was to walk herself right into his tormenting trap.

'Do you know where the runaway lovers have gone?' The question came at her right out of the blue.

'No.' She shook her head.

'Do you know, then, how your hair catches fire in the sunlight coming in through the window behind you?'

That oh, so silky spoken observation flared her hair around her face as she spun around. 'For goodness' sake, will you stop playing this crazy game now?' she shrilled out.

'No game,' he denied, and he was lounging in the chair now, so damn sure of himself and everything he'd dared to say to her that she couldn't take her eyes off him, couldn't *not* be aware of the sensual pulse emanating from every part of his long, lean body—like a man with his desire on the rise. The half-lowered eyelids, the low burning glow of gold in his eyes. The mouth that had softened to show its capacity for enjoying the pleasures of the senses and the challenge in his expression that wasn't really a challenge but a heat-seeking message of absolute promise.

'Marry me next week and I will lift your sex life from the disappointingly mundane to the bone-melting exciting,' he offered.

Lizzy gaped. 'Who told you my sex life was—?'

'Bianca, who else?'

Her best friend, *Bianca,* had said that about her—to him?

'She gave you two different lovers, neither of which lasted beyond the first venture between the sheets. Englishmen, of course,' he said, 'with a fumbling lack of finesse.'

'And you think speaking to me like this shows finesse?' The heat of dismay and the sharp sting of hurt were crawling all over her. She had never felt so let down by Bianca in their ten year friendship! How dared she speak to him about Lizzy's personal life—how dared she tell such wicked lies about it? 'Well I don't,' she said grimly. 'And I am not going to listen to any more of it.'

She turned—once again to leave.

But that relentlessly cool voice was not going to let her go. 'Marry me next week and I will bail your father out of debt, pay off his *loan* and send in my own team of experts to help oversee the recovery of his company,' it continued, bringing her to yet another quivering standstill. 'Which,' he added, 'I will fund until it can stand on its own two feet. *Don't* marry me next week, and I will light the litmus under an embezzlement scandal then just stand back to watch it go up.'

The bottom line, Lizzy recognised, the very lowest point he was prepared to go to to save his pride.

'Someone owes me, Elizabeth,' he went on grimly. 'Either

you pay the debt or your family pays that debt. The fact that I desire you is the only thing giving you the luxury of choice.'

'This is just revenge,' she whispered.

'Revenge is a form of passion, *mi amore*. My advice would be to grab my offer while the passion for revenge still rides hot in my blood.' Words...he was clever with words. So clever he was tying her head and her emotions into knots. Moving in a daze, she went to stand in front of one of the windows, staring out at the glittering lake backed by the misty grey mountains in the distance and the town of Bellagio just a simmering cluster of white on the opposite bank of the lake.

So near yet so far away, she thought bleakly. She could be marooned on an island with Luc as her jailor. As he'd already pointed out, she wasn't going anywhere without his express say-so.

And Matthew, she considered. Why had he done it? He was older than her, but only by eighteen months, and he'd had good reason to resent their father for his strict refusal to accept that his son had a right to choose what he wanted to do with his own life. Had he taken the money in an angry desire to hit back at their father? Had Bianca encouraged him to do it because it was his father who'd put a stop to their romantic plans to marry two years ago?

Mrs Moreno had told Edward Hadley that he was tackling their romance the wrong way. Ban them from seeing each other and you will create Romeo and Juliet, she'd warned in her dramatic way.

Dramatic or not, it appeared now that what she had predicted had come true—or at least partly true. Lizzy hoped to goodness that the two of them were not going to go the whole hog and drink poison.

But to take things as far as they already had done seemed fantastical to Lizzy, especially when she knew that both of them had been involved in other relationships since their break-up—the most important one being the one involving this man sitting here waiting for her answer.

And, she was going to have to admit it, she was hurt that neither of them had confided in her. Though maybe that part was not so fantastical because she would have tried to stop them and they would have known it.

'What will happen to them when they eventually resurface?' she questioned huskily.

'Bianca has done nothing wrong other than to change her mind about marrying me—a woman's prerogative,' he dryly pointed out. 'As it stands for your brother right now, it has to be up to your father and the bank to say what will happen to him.'

Smooth, blunt and honest. He didn't even bother to repeat that he was the one holding the axe suspended over Matthew's head.

Or she was.

'I won't wear Bianca's wedding dress,' she whispered. 'I won't marry you in a church. I won't let you buy me anything that isn't absolutely essential for the role you want me to play for you. And I won't stop working, because I need to earn money to pay you back every penny you invest in Hadley's.'

'You *will* marry me just as everything has been arranged already,' he countered. 'You *will* accept with grace anything I choose to bestow on you and you will *not* go back to work.'

Lizzy swung to face him and was shocked by the kick she received low in her gut because he was so— 'Y-you can't just slot me into Bianca's place just like that,' she said as she attempted to override over what her body was trying to make her feel. 'The authorities won't allow it!'

'At the risk of sounding boringly repetitive, money talks.'

Money talks. And so it did. 'I think I hate you,' she whispered.

'Nevertheless you will take up Bianca's place with pride and dignity and fool the world into thinking it was you and I and not them who discovered they couldn't live without each other. And you will *not* pay me back anything other than with our first child seeded in your womb. With that goal in mind you will come to our marriage bed with warmth and honesty—which means you will not fight against what we both desire.'

'Can I please go now?'

She was so close to tears she was barely managing to hold herself together and, the choked request brought a soft curse biting at the back of his throat. He came to his feet, made a move as if he was going to come towards her, then abruptly pulled himself up.

'In a moment.' The lean, handsome shape of his face had drawn into a cold, hard, impenetrable mask again. 'We have a few more details left to discuss.'

'Discuss?' Lizzy picked up. 'Doesn't that imply that I'm allowed an opinion?'

'Probably—' he grimaced '—but seemingly you are not, because I was about to say that I prefer to speak to your father before you do. Not up for discussion,' he added when she went to speak. 'Also, you will not be returning to the hotel in Milan because you will be living right here from now on.'

Lizzy pressed her fingers to her lips to try and stop them from trembling. 'Like a prisoner.'

'No,' he denied that. 'I can protect you here from the

fallout about to hit us when I make the announcement later today, whereas the hotel in Milan will be put under siege. I also have an itchy suspicion that the Morenos are not going to like this turn in events. You will feel sorry for them. I, on the other hand, will not.'

'What a joke.' She laughed thickly. 'Why do you think they delegated the job of coming here to me?'

Surprise momentarily lit his golden eyes up. 'So they're scared. Good, that works in our favour.'

'Will you stop talking as if this has anything to do with me when it hasn't?' Lizzy choked. 'I'm just the pawn here you're using to salve your wounded arrogance!'

'Pawns are very powerful pieces on the chessboard.'

'Oh, shut *up*!' she flared up. 'Have you *no* idea how infuriating it is that you have a slick answer to everything?'

'Seemingly not.' A hint of a wry smile touched the corners of his mouth. 'I will try to curb the habit,' he offered.

Pulling in a deep breath, Lizzy let it out again. '*Now* can I go?' she repeated.

Reaching out for the telephone sitting on his desk, he stabbed in a set of numbers, then began shedding instructions in Italian to whoever was listening on the other end while Lizzy listened and wished to God that she didn't find the rich smooth tones in his voice so attractive when he spoke his native language.

'Did you understand any of that?' he asked a moment later.

'Some.' She nodded. Having Bianca as a friend meant she'd learned to speak Italian pretty well over the years. 'You were arranging a room for me.'

'It will be ready in a few minutes.'

Stepping around the desk, he began walking towards her. Lizzy immediately tensed up, sheer instinct placing her onto the balls of her feet like a runner waiting for the sound of the gun.

'W-what?' she said warily when he pulled to a stop in front of her.

He said nothing, just held her eyes with one of his disconcertingly steady looks and lifted up a hand to her cheek with a crazily disturbing gentle touch. Lizzy released a broken little gasp, one part of her wanting her to jerk back from him, but another part refusing to let her give in to it when it would only tell him things she didn't want him to know.

And he was beautiful, there was just no denying it even though she very much wished that she could. For all of his coldness and his arrogance, his ruthless determination to have his way and the grim anger she instinctively knew was still stirring away behind the control, Luc De Santis possessed a physical beauty that was just so dangerously compelling.

His eyelids drooped as he moved his fingers to gently touch the corner of her mouth. 'I will make you a deal,' he said in the husky dark tones of a man about to get really personal. 'You can pay me back the money you owe me with kisses. Let's say—one kiss a euro,' he suggested. 'Starting from now…'

His dark head lowered and his lips parted, his fingers sliding to curve around her nape beneath the heavy fall of her hair.

Push him away, her one single working brain cell was screaming at her, but she remained perfectly still, tingling inside and breathlessly fascinated by the expression on his face as it came ever closer to hers.

A soft, helpless breath prized her lips apart, he scooped it away with the lick of his tongue, then he was kissing her, crushing his lips against her lips, warm and soft and undeniably—nice.

Then he was drawing back a little, searching her eyes to check out her response. 'Grey,' he murmured and grimaced. 'I am going to have to do better than that.'

He lowered his head again, long fingers guiding the tilt of her face to accept his second kiss and this time the sensual thrust of his tongue. Heat flared inside her for a second, and she was dimly aware of making a helpless groan.

Once again he withdrew. 'Almost green,' he said, 'and that makes two euros repaid to me.'

Then he smiled a brief smile, let go of her face and turned to stride away, pulling the door open and closing it behind him again, leaving Lizzy standing there, numbed by the knowledge that she'd just given him, free and for nothing, all the proof he needed that what he'd said about her wanting him was true.

She had no resistance to fight him with. She had been struggling with her attraction to him for weeks. And she did go up like a flame when he kissed her. Even if the flame had been only brief—it had happened. He'd felt it. As far as he was concerned their deal was sealed.

CHAPTER FOUR

THE MEDIA went into a frenzy. Lizzy learned, reluctantly, to be thankful that Luc had shown the foresight to move her into his home. No one was allowed near the villa without his express permission. No one was allowed to contact her by phone.

Except for her father. When Lizzy was eventually allowed to contact him she found him hurt and angry and confused. He couldn't believe that she of all people could put herself between her best friend and the man Bianca was supposed to marry. He was disappointed in her. 'I tell you, Lizzy, I hope you're not taking a leaf out of your mother's book.'

It had been the ultimate criticism that made her cringe in shame.

Matthew, on the other hand, had at last done something to earn their father's respect because—apparently—he'd chased over to Milan and taken poor Bianca away before the scandal hit the press. No, he had not heard from her brother. No, he had no idea where they'd gone.

And, most amazing of all, he hadn't a clue that Matthew had emptied the company bank account. 'An error,' he called it when she dared to broach the subject, 'which the bank put right the very next day.'

Even Luc came in for her father's reluctant respect because he'd been so ready to apologise for the distress they had caused so many people. And, of course, Luc was going to make recompense helping Hadley's to get back on its feet.

Only Lizzy was to be left out in the cold and his comparison to her mother told her why. But, yes, of course he would be there to give her away on Saturday. Luc expected it.

Good old Luc, Lizzy thought bitterly.

And as for the Morenos, they had a field-day talking to the press and telling them how their poor daughter's best friend had stolen Luc away.

'I'm a marriage-wrecker,' she informed the root of her character assassination via the telephone while she paced angrily up and down in front of his desk. She was speaking to Luc via the phone because after he'd walked out of here three days ago he had left the villa altogether and had not bothered to come back. 'Matthew is the saving knight on the white charger. Bianca is the betrayed damsel he saved. And you,' she told him, 'are the absolute epitome of man's idea of a man. Big enough to acknowledge your mistake in your choice of bride and arrogant enough to grab the one you decided you wanted instead!'

He laughed. Lizzy wanted to fly at him in a rage but he wasn't here and—what difference would it make if he were? She would still be all the bad things people were saying about her and...

'When you said I would be the one to carry the can, you really meant it,' she whispered.

'Once the fuss has died down you will become the envy of every woman out there, trust me,' he drawled.

'Because I've been fortunate enough to catch you?' That was just so typically arrogant of him! 'Well, I don't feel fortunate. I feel unforgivably used. So if you're expecting me to sign this prenuptial contract your lawyers have just delivered here, then you go to hell, Luc, because I'm not signing anything!'

With that she slammed down the phone.

He arrived at the villa a short hour later. Lizzy was in her room. It was a beautiful suite with views over the lake and a balcony she dared not step onto because of the million cameras trained on the windows from the ton of boats moored out there on the lake.

Curled up on a sofa reading a book that had no words printed on the pages as far as Lizzy could tell, she said 'Go away,' without looking at him.

He slammed the contract down on her lap. 'Sign,' he commanded.

Lizzy ignored him. She was wearing a short blue cotton skirt and a little lemon top, the sunlight coming in through the long window behind her setting the twisting mass of untidy curls on fire around her shoulders and face. She wore no make-up and she wore no shoes. And if any man was used to seeing his women primped to an eyelash it was Luciano Genovese Marcelo De Santis.

A really impressive proper fountain pen arrived on the top of the prenuptial contract. 'Sign,' he repeated.

Toying idly with a spiralling curl, Lizzy shifted her lips into a stubborn purse.

On a heavy sigh he turned and strode away from her. She heard the rustle of clothes. Reluctantly allowing herself a glance in his direction, she saw the jacket to an iron-grey suit land on the back of a bedside chair. By the time he turned back to face her, his tie had been loosened from around the collar of his blue striped shirt and her stomach muscles curled and stung.

The man meant business—she could tell by the look of determination she glimpsed on his lean, sleek honey-gold face before she quickly looked away.

He came back to where she was sitting with her long bare legs curled beneath her and the contract still resting across her thighs. Glancing around him, he reached out for a pretty pale blue brocade chair and brought it close to the sofa, then sat down.

'Listen,' he said, leaning forward to rest his forearms on his elegantly clad knees. 'I cannot marry you unless you sign the prenuptial agreement.'

'Shame,' Lizzy drawled, unperturbed, 'because I don't agree with it.'

He pulled in a breath. 'It is purely a business necessity,' he explained, keeping his voice deliberately level and calm. 'I am the head of a very prestigious bank. I am also worth more than a king's fortune. If you don't sign this my shareholders will lose confidence in me for being too weak to protect myself.'

'Then don't tell them,' Lizzy said rationally.

'They will find out. Things like this inevitably get out,' he reasoned. 'You will be judged a greedy gold-digger and I will be judged a fool.'

'So I will be judged a greedy gold-digging marriage-breaker.' Lizzy shrugged. 'What's one more label when I'm already covered in them?'

His hand snaked out. He took the book from her fingers and grimly tossed it aside. Next he picked up the fountain pen and held it under her nose.

'Sign,' he insisted.

Lizzy stared at the pen but didn't take it.

'Please,' he added.

She released a sigh. 'Strike out the bit about who gets the children in the event of a divorce,' she said heavily.

Without uttering a single word in protest Luc picked up the contract, found the relevant clause and struck lines through with the pen and even added his signature in a bold, sure, elegant scrawl.

'Now do the same with the one about me getting— whatever amount you've had put in there,' she murmured.

'No,' he refused.

'Take it or leave it,' Lizzy warned stubbornly.

'Then I will leave it.' He stood up with the contract and walked away. 'Our marriage is off. You have an hour to pack your things and get out of my villa, Miss Hadley,' he informed her. 'Take my advice and leave by the servant's entrance if you don't want to be swamped by the waiting press. Oh, and don't forget to tell your father that he owes me five and a half million pounds and the bank another five and a half million pounds.'

With that he hooked up his jacket and headed to the door.

Lizzy shot to her feet. 'All right, I'll sign!' she snapped, furious with herself for taking it so far that she'd lost the higher ground.

He paused, all lean, dark, sexy male with a way of holding himself that made Lizzy hate the trickle of awareness she felt heating up her insides.

He turned, that, oh, so clever face revealing absolutely nothing but cool authority as he walked back to her, dropped his jacket on the back of his vacated chair, then silently handed her the contract and the pen.

Spinning away, Lizzy stepped up to a little table by the window and scrawled her signature, then spun back to hand him the contract and the pen.

He took them in his long brown fingers—then calmly dropped them on the floor. The next thing she knew she was locked in his arms. Her shocked exclamation earned her nothing but the fierce pressure of his mouth and the hot, hard, probing thrust of his tongue. In the dim distant swell of her own pounding heartbeat, she was aware of the hunger he fed into that kiss and the tension locked into his hard-muscled frame. One of his hands took rough hold of her hair while the other was a clamp on her hip that kept her pressed tightly up against him.

And if she had never experienced the full force of a man's passion before, then she was learning all about it now. He kissed her deeply until she whimpered; he let her feel the growing power of his desire. He muttered something when she trembled against him, then he swung her off her feet and carried her to the bed.

'*Don't,*' she choked out when he lowered her down there and looked as if he was going to follow.

But he didn't follow. He stood there looking down at her, making her feel small and weak and very vulnerable as he flicked the burning gold heat of his gaze over the hectic rise and fall of her breasts and her tensely curling bare toes.

Those eyes came back to her eyes, then dropped to the reddened swell of her mouth. 'That's three euros paid off your debt to me, Miss Hadley,' he informed her coolly and turned, went to recover the prenuptial contract, his pen and his jacket, and strode out of the door.

But not without Lizzy seeing the heat that streaked across

his high cheekbones, or the visible signs of his arousal he'd found impossible to control. Curling up on the bed, she hugged herself and wished she understood what was making her tick these days. Wished she understood why watching him lose his unflappable control had excited her so badly she had to press her thighs together in a futile attempt to smother the sensation.

A helicopter arrived to transport her to her wedding. Shiny white and sparkling, it landed on the stretch of lawn that overlooked the lake. That morning a famous designer had arrived from Milan bringing her wedding gown. He was the first person she had seen besides Luc and the household staff for a week. She knew her father was here in Italy because she'd spoken to him on the phone. She knew that Luc was staying not far away because she'd seen a different helicopter with the De Santis logo glinting gold on his tail fly over the villa twice a day.

And she knew she was still the centre of a media frenzy because a maid had told her, giggling and excited about it, whereas all Lizzy could think was—how was she going to cope when her secure haven here in the villa had been taken away?

The gown bore no resemblance whatsoever to the one that Bianca had been going to wear, she was relieved to discover.

And it was truly beautiful. She hadn't a clue how the designer had managed to make it to fit her so perfectly and refused to ask the question, but the romantic drift of floating white silk made in the Grecian style disturbed her oddly when she viewed the finished effect in the mirror because she looked so soft and sensually curvy and—vestal.

Luc's idea of how a bride should look?

'Don't chew your bottom lip like that, *signorina*,' the designer advised with a critical frown. 'Your mouth is ripe enough to drive Luciano crazy without you plumping it up some more.'

Lizzy released her lip from her anxious white teeth and slithered her eyes over the silky fall of her hair. Carla the giggly maid had done it for her—washed it, conditioned it, actually almost tamed it. And the barely there hint of make-up applied by Carla's steady fingers made her look—

'It is now no mystery to me why he risked ridicule to replace *la bella Bianca* with what I see standing here,' the designer said.

'Don't,' Lizzy responded, her voice sounding shaky and thick the way it left her tense aching throat.

Her loyalty to her best friend would not allow anyone to mock Bianca. And she missed her. She wanted to see her, talk to her, find out why she'd run away with Matthew, and if what Lizzy was about to do had her blessing because if it didn't…

Lizzy swallowed, the ache of tears threatening her eyes. A knock at the door revealed Luis the major-domo who'd first led her into this villa a long week ago.

'It is time to leave, *signorina*,' he advised.

Her father met her at the church. He looked younger than he had when she'd left him in Sussex two weeks ago, the strain of worry having gone from his face, but the cold disappointment she saw in his eyes made her want to cry all the more.

'You look beautiful,' he said. 'Just like your mother.'

Just like her mother, Lizzy repeated bleakly as he bent to press a cool kiss to one of her cheeks.

Then he walked her into a church packed with curious witnesses. The rippling hiss of softly voiced comments accompanied them down the long stone aisle towards the man she could see standing tall and straight at the other end.

He was wearing morning grey—formal like her father, like the man standing beside him whom she vaguely recognized, but that was about as far as her ability to think about anything went.

And she wanted Bianca. Bianca was supposed to always have been here with her for her wedding just as she was supposed to have been there for hers.

And she wanted to stop and turn to her father and say sorry, beg his forgiveness because she couldn't bear knowing that he was walking beside her likening what she was doing here with what her mother had done ten years before.

The marriage-wrecker, the greedy little gold-digger only out to please herself. Being aware that she was just being silly believing her own press didn't help.

Then Luc turned to look at her, his lean, dark, sombre expression fixing on her like a magnet that pulled her the last few faltering steps to his side. Her father offered her hand to him, he took it, long brown fingers firm as they closed around the trembling state of her own. After that the rest became a hazy glaze of traditional solemnity wrapped in a muffling shroud of beautifully toned Latin that eventually joined them as man and wife.

And the kiss Luc pressed to her lips was somehow piercingly poignant if only because it sealed this mad, ill thought-out union in front of a few hundred fascinated witnesses.

Four euros, Lizzy found herself thinking as Luc lifted his mouth away again. It's going to take me a lifetime to pay back what I owe him.

As if he knew what she was thinking he grinned, all gleaming white teeth and mocking arrogance.

The next thing Lizzy became aware of was stepping out of the church into brilliant sunlight and a cacophony of sound. Cameras flashed, her heart fluttered into sudden panic, the man standing beside her drew her closer into his side. Two rows of dark-suited security men formed a barrier to hold back the curious onlookers and Luc hurried her down through this corridor of safety to a waiting limousine, his arm not leaving contact with her until he had seen her safely shut behind the car door.

The car sped off the moment he'd settled beside her. The hazy glaze lifted from her eyes. Silence stung. It was over. She'd done it. She'd married her best friend's fiancé. The air sounded choked as it left her lungs.

'So you do remember how to breathe,' Luc's quietly sardonic voice said beside her.

Seems so, Lizzy thought without attempting to offer a reply.

Instead she looked down at her hand where a traditional gold band now adorned her slender white finger. Across the gap separating them a matching band glowed against the brown of his skin. She hadn't expected him to wear a ring too, it had come as a surprise when she'd been quietly instructed to place it on his finger.

But, like the church and its packed congregation, she presumed the rings were the same rings he had bought for his marriage to Bianca.

'I am not that insensitive,' he said coolly.

So he was reading her mind as if he owned it too now. 'And at least the dress was mine.'

She sensed his sharp look, the slight tensing of his muscles as he caught the bleakness threading her tone. 'You don't like the dress?'

Was he blind? 'I love it. It's the most romantic and beautiful wedding gown I've ever seen.'

'And you look beautiful in it—*bellissima*,' he extended huskily. 'No one watching you come down the aisle to me was left wondering why it was you I married today.'

'One more goal on your pride-saving agenda successfully accomplished?'

Lifting her chin, Lizzy looked at him for the first time since they'd kissed as man and wife—then instantly wished that she'd kept her eyes lowered because he looked so bone-shiveringly breathtakingly devastating and perfect—the true handsome prince she had bagged for herself by foul means.

A bitter little smile caught hold of her mouth. 'Well, don't look to me for congratulations because you're not going to get any,' she told him, turning her eyes away.

'You feel cheated,' he murmured.

Of what? Lizzy wondered. Of choosing her own wedding dress? In truth she felt cheated of a lot of things today, not least the given right to choose her own husband, or having her best friend there to share her day with her, or seeing pride, not disapproval, on her father's face.

A sigh shot from her. 'I've hurt and disappointed my father with all of this.'

'And now you are in danger of disappointing me.'

It was the way he said it that made Lizzy look back at him, wary tension uncoiling inside her when she saw the almost savage glint of anger hardening his face.

'We made a deal,' he reminded her grimly. 'One where

neither of us would deny the one basic ingredient that will make this marriage work.'

He meant the mutual attraction. Lizzy pulled in a breath, her lips parting in readiness to say something cutting about that, but he stopped the words by reaching across the gap to press a set of cool fingers over her mouth.

'Be careful, *la mia moglie bella*, that you don't talk yourself into trouble with that unruly tongue of yours,' he advised. 'Your father will recover from his disappointment once he begins to consider the good fortune our marriage has blessed him with,' he assured with hard cynical bite. 'Just as you will learn to get over your disappointment in me as your husband because I intend to see to it that you do with the first bed and opportunity we get. And,' he continued in a dark driven undertone without letting her eyes break contact with his, '*I* will recover from my disappointment in you when you stop feeling sorry for yourself and remember just who you are now, *Signora De Santis*. For this name makes you my wife, my lover, the future mother of my children and the gracious custodian of the De Santis good name.'

Wow, was all Lizzy could think when he finally fell into a simmering silence. Somewhere in this strange conversation they'd been having she'd hit a raw nerve when she hadn't thought he had any!

Lifting up her hand, she caught hold of his fingers and pulled them away from her mouth. 'That was really good,' she commended. 'Quite breathtakingly arrogant and right-fully proud of your mighty fine self, in fact, and it should really have put me squarely in my lowly place.'

'But it didn't?' He raised a questioning eyebrow.

Lizzy shook her head, aware that her heart was pounding

erratically, but unaware that she was still holding onto his fingers—or that those fingers had curled around hers.

'You are still the guy who blackmailed me into marrying you to salve your ravaged pride and I am still the woman you *paid* to salve that ravaged pride!'

'You believe that there are no other women out there who would have jumped eagerly into your shoes?'

'I would imagine there are hundreds,' Lizzy said coolly. 'But aren't you the one that told me you could not be bothered to hunt?'

'Quick.' He smiled—then tugged on her fingers. Next thing she was lying in a slither of bridal silk across his chest. Her surprised gasp had barely broken free of her lips before she received the full passionate onslaught of his kiss. And this time it was hot and hard and deeply probing, as if he was deliberately piling on the passion in each kiss by carefully calculated degrees. By the time he raised his head again Lizzy felt dazed and shaken, her breathing fast and thick. Her lips felt bruised and the way he ran a finger across their warm, pulsing surface was a source of mockery in itself.

'As you see,' he murmured softly, 'I still do not need to hunt.'

It was such a slap at the way she'd gone into the kiss without putting up a fight that Lizzy paled and scrambled off his lap. Her dress was dishevelled, and as she tried to smooth it with unsteady fingers she felt the sultry burn of his eyes as he watched her, felt the drumming pulse of his sexual domination and the worst feeling of all—his amusement.

'I did warn you once, *cara*, that I am more experienced at these games than you are,' he reminded her from his languid sprawl on the other side of the car. 'Be a little wiser and stop trying to take me on.'

The car slowed then, sending her eyes to the side window to see that they'd arrived back at the villa without her noticing. Though her biggest surprise was that she hadn't known there was a different way into the villa other than via the lake. Now a huge pair of heavy iron gates were in the process of swinging open. The car glided through them and on through extensive gardens to pull to a smooth halt beneath a covered portico to the side of the house.

She hadn't dared to come outside while she'd been staying here because she hadn't wanted any members of the press to snatch a picture of her from their siege position on the lake. But glancing towards the lake now as Luc helped her alight from the car, she was stunned to see that it was no longer there! All view of the lake had been totally blanked out by a wall of sturdy white canvas that had been erected along the cliff edge—she assumed to frustrate greedy camera lenses from taking pictures of the wedding celebration about to take place.

The whole celebrity-style over-the-top show intimidated her from that moment onward. If Bianca had been here Lizzy would have taken it all in her stride with a dose of healthy humour to help her along. But then if Bianca had been here, she would have been the bride at this wedding and taking the sparkling centre of attention as her due, with Lizzy happy to fade into the background, as she liked to do.

As it was, she wasn't allowed to fade anywhere. She had to stand beside her new husband and welcome their guests in from the church.

His guests, she reminded herself. *His* wedding day. None of her friends had been invited, just her father, whose disapproval still showed when he arrived and gave her a stiff hug.

Her eyes pleaded with him for understanding, but all he saw when he looked at her was a woman like her mother, and there was no forgiveness in him at all. It was like being deserted by her only ally and she found she had to fight back the tears as she watched him turn his back on her and walk away.

'Explain to me what the hell that was about,' the man standing beside her demanded.

But Lizzy just gave a silent shake of her head and blinked the tears away. A man like Luc would never understand what it felt like to be crushed beneath the weight of someone's disapproval. The feeling would be as alien to him as—as feeling uncomfortable with the sensation he'd caused with his quick change of bride! In all the years since her mother had left them, Lizzy had tried her best to show none of her wayward traits. But as she stood here now in this beautiful villa, wearing this beautiful gown, feeling so rejected by the one person she should have been able to rely upon for support, she had to ask herself if spending her life trying to earn her father's approval had just been a useless waste of her time.

And her now very crushed heart.

The endless stream of elegant guests kept on coming. She smiled, she endured the looks of cool interest, the polite comments and the sometimes not so polite. Hurt clung heavily to her chest while her face maintained its placid composure and Luc kept her close to him, with his arm strapped at an angle across her back so his hand could rest in the indentation of her waist.

Eventually they began to circulate. No one got to speak to either of them individually. His hand remained a firm clamp at her waist. He was showing a united front and no amount of teasing from his closer friends about his possessive attitude to his bride could budge him from her side.

They ate from a beautiful serve-yourself banquet—Lizzy nibbled sparingly, held her untouched glasses of bubbling champagne and endured the amused, mostly ironical speech from Luc's best man with her eyes carefully lowered, Luc with a wry but complacent smile on his face.

Nothing touched him, she noticed. The man had nerves of steel and no emotion at all. Yet she knew by the changing grip of his fingers on her waist that sometimes something violent erupted inside him, especially when they caught the edges of hushed conversations discussing Bianca and the fact that the poor jilted bride seemed to have slipped off the face of the earth.

Was his response due to anger or pain? When she glanced up at his face, it, of course, revealed nothing.

She caught fleeting glimpses of her father in the crowd and wanted to go and ask him if he'd heard from Matthew, but every time the thought hit, Luc was guiding her off in the opposite direction.

The afternoon wore on with agonising slowness until she began to really feel the strain of maintaining her smile. So when Luc bent his head to tell her quietly that it was time for her to go and change out of her dress, she was so pathetically relieved to be given an excuse to escape she didn't even bother to ask him why she needed to change.

Carla the giggly maid was waiting for her when she reached her bedroom. She provided the answers as she helped her out of her wedding dress.

'It is such a shame that you must remove this beautiful gown so soon, *signora*.' Carla sighed wistfully. 'But with your new clothes all packed in your bags and already on their way, it must be so exciting and romantic to be swept away by the *signor* to your secret honeymoon destination.'

Honeymoon—?

CHAPTER FIVE

OH, PLEASE don't, Lizzy thought helplessly, so horrified that Luc was intending to take this romantic stuff that far that her lips came together with a snap to stop the groaned protest from slipping out.

But the protest glowed in her eyes as she came back downstairs dressed in a soft green wraparound dress that clung lovingly to her figure and swirled around her knees.

Luc was already waiting at the bottom of the stairs for her. He had changed too, into a soft coffee-coloured linen suit and a simple tee shirt that made him look cool and casual and superbly stylish and just too darn sexy to be fair.

He looked up at her and something flared in his eyes that made her steps falter as her heart gave a fluttering stir. Then the expression was gone and he was holding out a hand in a silent command for her to continue down the rest of the stairs.

When she came close enough, he took hold of her hand and drew her towards him. His lips arrived at her temple; she felt the heat from his body warm against hers.

'Beautiful,' he husked.

So are you, Lizzy thought helplessly, but she didn't say it.

'Where are we going?' she whispered instead, sharply aware of all the people standing around watching them.

'Where all newly married couples go.' He took the cream jacket she had draped across her arm. 'Somewhere we can be alone.'

'But I don't want to be alone with you.' She frowned as he draped the jacket across her shoulders.

'You don't? I am devastated.'

He just sounded sardonic to her. 'I thought we would be staying here. Can't we just stay here?' She glanced up at him anxiously. 'I'm used to being here now. It's—comfortable.'

In the process of gently releasing her hair from inside the jacket, Luc paused to look down at her, a strange expression swirling around in his dark golden eyes.

Then the smile was back. 'It is traditional to change venue.'

Lizzy stepped a little closer to him, her voice a hurried confiding whisper aimed at the taut solid skin at his throat. 'It's silly.'

'What is?'

'The rest of this.' Her eyes gave a quick restless flick of the waiting crowd. 'If we're supposed to be leaving, won't *they* all be leaving too?'

'You want me to throw our guests out?' He sounded incredulous.

'Your guests,' Lizzy corrected.

'Watch it, *cara*,' he warned quietly. 'You don't want to talk yourself into yet another tight corner with me—especially with so many witnesses.'

'All I'm saying is that we might as well stay—'

He moved so smoothly she didn't sense it coming. One

second he was smoothing the jacket across her shoulders, the next his long fingers crushing the slender bones, and with a controlled strength he pulled her tight up against his chest and the rest of her argument was being thoroughly crushed by the kind of kiss that locked the breath in her throat.

She was only dimly aware of the murmuring ripple that spread around the hallway as the first tense quiver to hit her in days made its fierce stroke down Lizzy's front. Pleasure flared out from its edges, sending her hands up to press hard against his chest in an attempt to push him away. But he was going nowhere and neither was the kiss, the heated force of it sending her body into a straining arch against him. The so carefully draped jacket slithered from her shoulders to land on the ground by her feet and his arms folded her even closer—someone murmured something mocking, someone else uttered a dry laugh.

Luc eased the pressure on her mouth by slow degrees and with tender stroking caresses. 'The show must go on, *cara*,' he murmured softly.

Too shaken up by the whole public reminder, Lizzy just swallowed tensely and nodded. Then the slow-rolling swell of applause took off around the gathering as Luc was stepping back.

Stooping down to recover her fallen jacket, he tossed it casually over his shoulder as he straightened again, then turned to offer their audience a wry mocking bow. Laughter joined in with the clapping. Lizzy kept her eyes lowered and hated the wild blush that burned her cheeks.

It wasn't until he'd captured her hand and led her outside and she saw the helicopter standing on the lawn again that she remembered her father.

She turned quickly to Luc. 'I can't leave here without seeing my father.'

He tensed beside her. 'He has already left here to catch his flight back to Gatwick,' he informed her coolly.

For a whole minute Lizzy couldn't breathe. The sense of rejection was so total she just stared blindly at Luc as the colour slowly drained from her face.

With a soft curse, he drew her across the lawn and bundled her into the helicopter. A few minutes later and they were rising up above the temporary wall of white canvas and swinging round to face the lake where a whole armada of different sailing crafts clustered a short way out from the jetty, with their army of little media people scrambling, no doubt to get a picture of them leaving.

Beside her Luc made a tense, restless movement with his body. 'Ignore them,' he rasped. 'They will soon get tired of playing this game and move on to the next sensation.'

Oddly enough she didn't care any more how many silly photographs they managed to snatch.

'He left without saying goodbye to me,' she whispered.

That was what mattered.

'He has a business to rescue.' He didn't even try to pretend he did not know who she meant. 'You must accept that Hadley's has to take priority with him right now.'

Oh, yes. 'Thank you,' she said, 'for that very thin excuse.'

After that they finished the journey to the accompanying sizzle of his frowning impatience and her numbed silence. Lizzy stared out of the window as they skimmed over the top of the glistening blue lake. An hour later they were crossing the tarmac at Linate Airport to a private jet wearing the De Santis logo on its shiny white fuselage.

The interior was a luxurious statement to corporate living. Luc saw her seated, said something to a hovering steward, then strode off to check with his pilot.

Two minutes later he was back, and the engines were running. He took the chair next to Lizzy and clipped home his seat belt, instructing her to do the same thing.

They took off into pure blue skies and she still hadn't got a clue as to where they were going. In truth she just didn't care. Today had been the worst day of her life and right now she felt like a traffic accident, one of the walking wounded that functioned by sheer instinct and nothing else.

'I sent him away while you were changing,' Luc rasped out suddenly, bringing her face around to stare at him.

He was lounging in the seat beside her, the absolute epitome of casual nonchalance, but Lizzy saw the tension around his mouth.

'Why?' she breathed.

His golden eyes flickered over her. 'He upset you.'

He upset her? 'He's my father,' she snapped out. 'He's allowed to upset me!'

'I am your husband,' he countered. 'I am allowed to remove all upset from your life.'

Lizzy threw him a look of burning dislike. 'You upset me. Does that mean you're going to remove yourself from my presence?'

'Not while we are flying at ten thousand feet.' He grinned—then stopped grinning and sighed instead. 'Stop spitting hatred at me, Elizabeth, and explain to me why your father believes he can treat you the way that he did today.'

So she told him about her mother in a cool, flat, dignified voice, unaware that he watched every fleeting expression that passed across her face because she refused to look at him as she talked.

'So you see,' she concluded, 'he sees his worst fears for me materialising in our wedding today.'

The steward arrived then with coffee and sandwiches, bringing a halt to the conversation while he transferred everything from a tray to the low table in front of them. Luc waved the steward away when he went to pour out the coffee and leant forward to do it himself.

'Do you look like your mother?' he asked curiously.

Lizzy nodded. 'I'm like this constant reminder to him of what she did.'

He handed her a cup of warm dark coffee. 'And where is she now?'

'She—died, two years ago.' Her voice had turned so husky she took a sip at the coffee to cover it up—then frowned at the bitter sweet taste. 'You've put sugar in this.'

'You don't take sugar?'

'No,' she said—then, curiously, 'Do you?'

Sitting back in his seat, he took a sip from his own cup. 'We don't know very much about each other, do we?'

No, Lizzy thought bleakly, we don't. 'Well, do you take sugar in your coffee or don't you?' she demanded.

'Strong, black and sweet,' he answered, then turned his head to look at her, his golden eyes darker than usual and reflecting an expression she could not quite read.

But she felt it make its old strike at her solar plexus and frowned as to why it had. They couldn't be discussing a safer subject unless they switched to the weather.

'It seems to me, *cara*,' he then said ruefully, 'that your

family is as dysfunctional as mine, which makes us more in tune than you would like to think.'

Opening her mouth to argue with him, she closed it again, because she realised he was probably right. 'I still don't like sugar in my coffee,' she said firmly, and put her cup on the table.

He just laughed, and rang for the steward to bring another cup.

For some unknown reason her mood lightened. She even ate a couple of sandwiches and felt herself begin to relax.

'Where are we going?' she finally decided to ask him.

'Well, that took its time,' Luc mocked, getting up to stride down the cabin. 'The Caribbean,' he enlightened as he opened up what turned out to be a drinks cabinet and selected a bottle from the row. 'I have a place there, hidden away on a paradise island with only pelicans for company—want one?'

He turned to show her what looked like brandy. Lizzy shook her head.

'Scared you will get tipsy again?'

'Scared I'll fall asleep.'

'Fortunately for you—' he came back with two glasses and sat down again '—falling asleep on board this plane is not a problem because we have a bed to sleep in through that door you can see at the other end of the cabin.'

Expression as bland as he could make it, he waited for her nervous glance towards the door set into the bulkhead, then silently offered her a glass.

It was either take it or endure another round of sarcastic comments from him, Lizzy knew that.

'With a nine-hour flight ahead of us, with or without the brandy, you are going to discover a need for that bed.'

'With or without you?' It was out before she could stop it.

His golden eyes lit up. 'Was that an invitation?'

'No, it was not!' she denied.

'Then take the brandy,' he said. 'You are safe with me—for now.'

It was the *for now* that made her feel edgy, but it was the lazy challenge in his tone that made her take the brandy from him and defiantly toss it to the back of her throat.

'Not a good idea, *cara*,' he said as he watched her fall into a fit of gasps as the brandy burnt like fire all the way down to her stomach.

He was right and it wasn't. The brandy went straight to her head. She lasted a full long hard-fought-for hour before she succumbed to the need to lie down and close her dizzy eyes.

Luc offered to help her down the cabin. She refused with a stiff dignity that cost her plenty to make it all the way into the small bedroom without stumbling over her own feet.

A few minutes later, wearing only her bra and panties, she was curling up beneath a soft duvet covered in the smoothest linen, and dropping into a muzzy sleep with what felt like the world playing drumbeats on her head.

For hours she slept, she didn't know how many, before she came drifting upwards into semi-darkness with the muted sound of the plane's engines to remind her where she was.

Her head had cleared and she felt so much better than she'd felt when she'd come in here. She was hungry too, but the idea of getting up out of the comfortable bed and getting dressed to go out there and face Luc had her turning over in the bed with the intention of staying right where she—

Shock froze the air in her body when she saw him. He was lying on his front right beside her with his dark head resting on the pillow next to her pillow and his wide naked shoulders glowing bronze in the soft light coming from the lamp on his side of the bed.

From being completely relaxed to the point of a wonderful bonelessness, she was already in the process of tensing up when she realised he was asleep and she let the tension seep away again on an inner swirl of tingling relief.

The black satin crescents of his eyelashes were resting peacefully against his high cheekbones and his mouth was the most relaxed she had seen it, its sensual shape all the more beautiful in repose, and his hair was ruffled, revealing a hint of a glossy black wave she hadn't ever noticed before.

Held by a curiosity she knew she should not be giving in to, Lizzy let her eyes roam over his arms, thrown up against the pillow, the width of his shoulders and long bronzed back exposed because the duvet had slipped down so low.

Her fingers scrambled at her own part of the duvet, inching it carefully over her shoulder because his nakedness reminded her about her own near nakedness.

Was he naked—as in completely naked? The intimacy of the situation struck like a feather being drawn across the surface of her skin. Her nostrils flared and she picked up the warm scent of him, clean yet so irresistibly male it sent the moist tip of her tongue sliding on a slow circuit of her warm lips for a reason she refused to examine.

And the skin covering the muscles she could see shaping his body wore a sheen that made her think of suntan oil, though she knew the effect was due to his own natural oils conditioning his skin while he slept.

Her husband, she thought, trying the title out to see how it felt, and still found the concept as alien to her as having the two of them lying here together in this bed.

'Grey,' a deep, dark, slumberously warm voice murmured.

Lizzy started, her eyes leaping up to his face. He was awake. She tensed, her fingers gripping the duvet. She would have dived right out of the bed if she weren't aware that she was wearing the sheerest leaf green bra ever fashioned and matching panties that made a mockery of the name.

'Sexy soft smoky grey—no, don't move away,' he said when she went to do just that, and with a lithe shift of his body he rolled onto his side and propped his head on the heel of his hand so he could look down into her wary face and the scented fire flow of her hair where it spread across the pillow.

'*Bellissima,*' he chanted softly. '*La signora bella De Santis.*'

'No,' she denied. 'Will you stop calling me beautiful?'

'Strange creature.' He smiled, reaching over to stroke the stray curl from her brow. 'You have the most exquisite face I have ever seen on any woman and the most fascinating determination to deny it. I would love to know why that is.'

'I won't respond to your kind of flattery—' the curl flopped back again and Lizzy swiped at it frowningly '—just because you…'

Her voice trailed away, teeth pressing into her bottom lip when she realised what she had been about to say next.

Moving that bit closer to her so she felt the tingling sting of his chest hair prickle the skin on her arm, he prompted, 'Because I—what?'

'Because w-we're married and—here,' she finished—then shook out an unsteady gasp when one of his legs arrived across both of hers. 'W-what do you think you're doing?' she demanded.

'Getting comfortable with my wife.'

Her fingers let go of the duvet so she could use them to push him back again, but it came as a tingling shock to her racing senses to feel the solid heat of his muscled body and the crisp warmth of his chest hair prickle against her palms. The whole situation was a tingling shock, she decided, snared by the living warmth of his leg weighing heavy on hers and the expression in his eyes as he continued to look down at her, tender and soft and still sleepy enough to make those shadowing eyelashes diffuse the hunter-like gleam from the gold.

She could even feel the steady beat of his heart where he pressed against her arm. He leant down and kissed her, not passionately or anything, just light and gently, yet she still jerked her head back, feeling besieged by his heat and his strength and his close proximity.

'Stop panicking,' he chided softly. 'I am not here to hurt you.'

'But I don't—'

'And it is customary that you kiss the man you wake up with.'

He was expecting her to kiss him? No way, she thought, and gave him her response with a shake of her head.

'You mean you expect me to do the kissing? Not very fair of you, *cara*, but—okay,' he said, and his mouth found hers again, only this time he traced the outline of her lips with his tongue, then gently probed between until she gave in and parted them for him. She let him taste her with a sensual slowness, her breath trapped in her chest. By the time he pulled away again her heart was thumping heavily and her lips trembled in protest at the loss of his.

'Not a bad way to start the new day,' he murmured.

'It—it's still dark out there,' Lizzy managed to whisper.

'But past midnight,' he said, drawing back a little to rest his head on the heel of his hand again. 'You were asleep for hours. You missed our first dinner together as man and wife and left me alone to contemplate the folly in urging my temperate bride to knock back brandy like a fully-fledged alcoholic.'

Lizzy flushed. 'Being unused to drinking brandy does not make me temperate.'

'Intemperate, then?'

Meaning she'd behaved like a hot-headed fool? He was probably right, she accepted reluctantly.

'Well, I'm hungry now,' she said with what she congratulated herself as sounding near normal with her heart still thumping against her ribs. 'S-so if you would just move your leg away I'll get up and…'

Her voice faded into nothing at the slow shake of his head. 'Relax,' he encouraged. 'I am not going to seal our wedding vows here in this very unromantic place, but I do want some more of what we have been sharing…a lot more,' he husked as he lowered his head again, and this time there was nothing slow or gentle about it.

His mouth claimed her mouth with deep, sweet, sensual male hunger, and he pressed her back into the pillows with the weight of his body, driving the breath from her lungs. Heat poured into every skin cell, the taste and the scent of him and the ravishing passion making her lose her death grip on the duvet so her hands could clutch at him for dear life.

His husky assurance that he was not going to turn this into something she wasn't ready for gave her the excuse she needed to just let go of restraint and she began kissing him back with an eager fervour, her body arching into the pressure of his. She barely noticed when he stripped the duvet away altogether; she just writhed with pleasure when she felt his hand stroke the length of her pale naked thigh.

Dragging his mouth from hers, he burned a dark golden look into her eyes. 'You feel like silk,' he breathed, the words deep and excitingly unsteady.

Then he made her groan when he reclaimed the kiss, his hand stroking upwards over the thin line of her panties to the flat of her stomach, the warmth of his skin against her over-sensitised skin making her quiver and cling as he blazed a trail of burning possession over her taut, slender ribcage to the rounded thrust of her breasts.

Panic arrived in a self-conscious rush from her exposed thighs to her throat as he gently cupped his fingers around the firm, rounded fullness of her breast barely covered by the green flimsy mesh of her bra. She tried to push his hand away, but he caught hold of her wrist with his other hand, making the flurrying sound of her breath shiver from her body as he gently lifted her hand out of the way so he could sear a path of warm, moist kisses down the arching column of her throat and over the hectic pant of her other breast.

She cried out and went wild beneath him as the sensual lap of his tongue located her nipple, sending a clamouring shock of heat piercing sensation screaming through her head.

With a softly uttered tense expletive he came back to her mouth, his hand sliding beneath her to draw her up against him. The next thing she knew the clasp of her bra had sprung free and he was lying her back against the pillows again and the scrappy bit of mesh was being trailed away.

'You are exquisite,' she heard him rasp through the hazy mists of her ravaged senses.

Then he was taking her mouth once again, crushing the

pulsing hot softness of her lips and dipping deep and hungrily with his tongue at the same time that his hand closed around her breast again, naked now and so alive to his touch she cried out in half protest, half sense spinning pleasure, and grabbed blindly at his head, her fingers clawing into the glossy thickness of his hair.

He kneaded and shaped and kissed her breathless. She could feel the tremors attacking him, feel the fevered flush of his body and the tension in him, trapped his groan with her tongue when he pressed the distended tightness of her nipple against his palm.

She should have stopped it there, but she didn't. She should have known that if you arched and writhed and quivered against a man you were going to tip him over the edge. But she liked what he was making her feel, too much, and was much too greedy for more.

And his hands were gliding everywhere now, caressing and learning what made her cry out and what made her writhe in shimmering pleasure. And his skin was like hot satin against her anxiously restless palms. She had never felt so totally out of control of her body and senses. She was panting and whimpering against his mouth and he was breathing fast and unevenly.

Reality should have arrived with the burgeoning thrust of his powerful erection pushing against her thigh at the same moment as he slid his hand between her legs and made that final intimate claim—but reality was nowhere. She was lost in a storm of heated pleasure. It sang along her veins and her flesh and it was all she could do to cling to him as his long fingers cupped and moved against her, his other hand buried in her hair, and the heat of his kiss was so deep and potently passionate she was almost beyond recovery when he lifted his mouth to mutter, 'I knew you would do this to me,' and eased her last scrap of mesh out of his way so he could glide the length of a finger inside.

Nothing prepared her for the power of this heated intrusion. There was just no way she could control her response. She arched and squirmed and found her mouth locking onto his as if it were the only way she was going to survive what was racing through her blood. He was whispering things she couldn't hear, and filling her with sensations she hadn't known she could feel.

Then he moved to strip the panties from her body and it was the rasping curse he uttered that brought her crashing back down to earth.

Panic erupted from her like a heaving monster, and she pushed him away from her with the agonised strength helped by the stinging shot of adrenalin singing through her blood. She caught a glimpse of his face, his shocked confusion, then she'd slithered out from beneath him to land in a mess of shaking limbs and whirling senses on her feet by the bed.

The pulsing silence that followed held the small cabin in a death grip except for the sound of her broken breathing. Her eyes felt so big and dark and glazed she was barely even able to see him through them.

'Y-you said—' she finally just about managed.

'I know what I said,' he coolly cut in.

Lizzy blinked, her eyes daring to focus on him still lying there with his long body so magnificently naked to his long brown feet. He had covered his eyes with an arm and the mouth beneath it was closed and tight. Unable to stop her eyes from raking over him, she stared at the potent evidence of his desire thrusting up from a thick cluster of virile dark hair.

Shocked by the blinding rush of heat that burned through her, she turned dizzily away with absolutely no idea what she was going to do next.

Jump on him, a wicked voice inside her suggested. 'Oh, God,' she choked, lowering her head to cover her burning eyes with her hands. She couldn't believe she'd ever let it go that far—she couldn't believe she'd trusted the promise he'd made!

'You have the sexiest backside,' he drawled suddenly, making the tumble of her hair slither down her spine as she arched upright. 'Creamy white and smooth and tight and deliciously framed by the lace edges of your pretty useless pants.'

Feeling the sting of total embarrassment, Lizzy reached behind her to hook the green mesh back into its rightful place.

'You think that helped?' he mocked.

She shook her head and wished she still had her bra on, because she just might have found the courage to turn around and spit something vile at him. But she didn't and her breasts felt heavy and throbbed, the fiercely distended tips stinging like aliens with the power to reach down deep inside her and pluck at other senses she wished she didn't have.

'You think, then, it is good fun to call a stop when things were becoming—passionate?'

He was angry. It hit Lizzy like a blow that arched her aching spine some more. 'Y-you don't understand.'

'I know a tease when I encounter one,' he said cynically.

She heard movement behind her to say he was getting off the bed, and like a wild thing she snatched up the only thing she had available—her wraparound top, which she dragged on. He too was pulling his clothes on; she could hear the rustle as she wrapped the top around her and tied it in an angry, tight, finger—trembling knot.

'A man who can't honour his promises deserves to be switched on—and off,' she responded once she felt safer to do it with her upper body covered up.

'No natural instincts at work in you, then,' he scorned that.

Snatching up her skirt and shimmying into it, she finally felt brave enough to turn around. He was standing on the other side of the bed, with the bulkhead almost touching his broad shoulders. And he was still so boldly naked she wished her ravished senses would just curl up and die. The soft light from the bedside lamp played across the flexing muscles in his shoulders as he pulled on his trousers, the taut clench of stomach and his hair-roughened chest.

Dragging her eyes away from him, she missed the way he lowered his own eyes to the burgeoning fullness of her breasts moulded by fine knit fabric so the tight peaks of her nipples pushed against the cloth.

'I'm not going to apologise for calling a stop to what you said was not going to happen,' she tossed back her hair and said.

He hooded his eyes, the old cold cynicism back with a vengeance. Bending down towards the bed, he picked up something. 'Here…' He tossed it at her. 'You had better put this on before you walk out of here, or my steward will suffer an apoplectic fit.'

With that ruthless cut into her bravery, he pulled the black tee shirt on over his head, then strode towards the door. It didn't slam—it wasn't designed to slam, Lizzy realised as she watched it seal into place.

But he'd wanted it to slam, the grim, spoiled, arrogant devil.

Then she looked down at the bra she now held in her fingers, glanced at her body and blushed to the roots of her hair.

They finished the rest of the journey in a state of cool withdrawal from each other scattered with super-polite snatches of conversation now and then. Lizzy ate, he didn't, instead he drank coffee, and no hint of alcohol in any form put in an appearance.

Eventually he produced a bulging briefcase and settled into his chair to concentrate—Lizzy wished she had something similar so that she could do the same thing.

But she didn't. She was now the pampered wife of a very rich man and her job as her father's secretary had gone. Her new role in life was to look the part of a rich man's wife—learn to look the part, she amended. And to be quiet when the rich husband was concentrating, because the look on his stern profile told her that was what he expected her to do.

Eventually she dozed again, curled into her seat with her shoes slipped off and her feet tucked beneath her and her head resting against the corner of the chair. When she awoke it was to find herself covered with a soft blanket and Luc was still sitting beside her working away.

She watched him for a while, sleepy eyes following the sudden flick on his pen when he scrawled something on the document he was reading, long fingers deft and supple and precise in their link with his brain. It was the same fountain pen she'd used to sign the prenuptial contract, she noticed, black, with a ring of gold circling its slender body, the platinum tipped nib feeding ink onto the paper like liquid silk.

'You've spelt indecisive wrong,' she murmured without knowing she was going to say it, or even that she'd been reading as he wrote.

The pen stopped and lifted. He turned to look at her,

golden eyes not angry any more, just coolly detached. 'I do not misspell,' he informed her arrogantly.

'You've used an "i" instead of an "e",' she insisted. 'The sentence says, "This attitude is indecisive and unaccceptable."' she read aloud. 'It loses impact with the misspelling.'

'You can read my writing from right over there?' Setting his shoulders against the back of his chair, he looked at her curiously. 'To the point that you can distinguish an "i" from an "e"?'

Lizzy nodded, still curled beneath the blanket. 'Not if you were writing in Italian,' she felt she should point out. 'My Italian spelling isn't good enough.'

'Nor is your English.'

Lizzy glanced at his face. There wasn't a flicker of uncertainty in his expression, yet she hadn't seen him look down to check if she was right. Which meant that either he was too confident for his own good, or she had made a mistake.

Uncurling her feet from beneath her, she pushed aside the blanket and reached out and took the page from his lap. She read it carefully, then handed it back to him without uttering a single word.

His eyelashes flickered, uncertainty darkening the colour of his eyes, and she laughed softly, couldn't help it—it felt so very good to be right.

He looked down, couldn't help himself, then a rueful smile stretched his lips. 'You aggravating ginger haired witch,' he said, having to carefully turn an 'i' into an 'e'.

'My hair's not ginger,' Lizzy protested.

'What is it, then?' Tossing the work down on the table in front of them, he sat back and looked at her again.

'Chestnut,' Lizzy answered, and combed a set of fingers

through it to push the curls away from her face. 'With a will of its own,' she added as a curl flopped down onto her brow.

'Much like its owner.'

'So you noticed.' She gave the errant curl another hopeless swipe only to watch it spring back down again.

'I noticed,' he answered evenly.

'Have you also noticed yet that I'm a virgin?' she asked him casually.

CHAPTER SIX

IF LIZZY said it to shock Luc out of his cool composure, then she certainly succeeded, she saw, as burning dark colour swept across his high golden cheekbones and he launched to his feet sending paperwork scattering as he accidentally knocked against the table.

'Is that your idea of a damn joke?' His eyes flashed out a blaze of blistering fury that made her reach for and pull up the blanket.

'I just—thought I should mention it before things go too— heated again,' she explained, blushing herself because now that she'd said it she felt silly and stupid and—

'A virgin,' he snapped out from between his clenched teeth. 'Where the hell did you get the idea to throw something like that at me from out of nowhere?'

'Well, what would you have preferred me to do?' Lizzy reacted hotly. 'Have it written into that stupid prenuptial contract so you could take your time getting used to the idea?'

He was pale with anger now, not flushed. 'We just almost made love—'

'No, I stopped it,' she reminded him, 'being such a horrible tease.'

Grabbing the back of his neck, he spun away from her. Lizzy huddled in her seat. 'I was going to tell you before in— in the bedroom but you turned nasty. Now I wish I hadn't told you at all!'

'So do I,' he muttered, striding off towards the drinks cupboard.

'Well, if it offends you this much, then why don't you do your usual trick and chuck this bride out and put another more experienced one in her place?'

'It does not offend me,' he denied stiffly. 'And I did not chuck Bianca out, as you so charmingly put it. She left me.'

'Wise girl,' Lizzy choked, fighting hurt tears now because hearing him say that made her remember that she wouldn't be here having this conversation if Bianca hadn't walked away from him.

Bianca, his first-choice bride!

'Well…' getting up, she began picking up scattered papers because she desperately needed something to do '—I am what I am, and you are what you are, which says to me that we don't have m-much going for us in this stupid m-marriage. But I know I can't bury my head in the sand and pretend I'm going to stop you every time you touch me because we both know I like it too much!'

'Elizabeth—'

'No,' she choked out. 'Just sh-shut up, because hearing you toss out one of your clever answers right now will just m-make me sick!'

He actually looked startled. 'I was not about to—'

'Yes, you were. You don't know how not to.' Swiping the tears from her eyes and that annoying stray curl from her brow, she gathered in his papers with trembling fingers, then came to her feet. 'I don't know how to deal with a man like you and it's making this situation very difficult for me.'

'You think I know how to deal with you?' he hit back. 'You are nothing like any woman I've ever encountered.' He knocked his drink to the back of his tense throat. 'You are quiet and shy and unbelievably sensitive in one disguise, then a flaming mix of defiance and passion in another!'

'Well, now you know why.' She put the papers on the table.

'Yes, I know why,' he accepted. 'You're a virgin—'

'Trapped in a marriage I didn't want.'

'By a man that you *do* want.'

Lizzy swallowed thickly because she just had no defence to that. She did want him, even though she wished that she didn't. She had wanted him for so long the guilty feeling still creased her insides.

'I'm not going to fool myself that you really want me,' she responded unsteadily, hunting around for her shoes now, though where the heck she thought she was going to go in them she hadn't a clue. 'Like you so love to say, you don't hunt and I'm here. But if you're daring to think that because I'm attracted to you I can't m-mind that I come in second best for you, then forget it, because I do mind.' She swallowed again. 'And the fact that I'm not being given the choice as to who I give my virginity to hurts enough without you responding as if I'm offering you some dreadful social disease.'

'I apologise if you feel I gave you that impression.'

He was coming over all cool and stiff now, which, Lizzy supposed, was typical of him.

'You—surprised me,' he added.

I surprised myself, Lizzy thought bitterly. I should have kept my big mouth shut.

'And if the—sex between us is such an issue to you, then perhaps we can take it more slowly from now on.'

So he didn't even want the sex with her now, Lizzy took from that smooth toned offer. 'Thank you,' she responded with chilly politeness.

The 'fasten seat belts' sign beeped into action then, saving her from the risk of sinking to the floor in a puddle of wretched tears. Instead she sat down, fastened her seat belt and occupied her trembling fingers by folding up the blanket.

A tinny voice came over the speaker system. 'We will be landing in five minutes, Luc. The weather is dry with humidity at seventy-five degrees. The time is—twenty-one thirty-three. Santo is waiting with your car.'

Luc closed the drinks cabinet with a telling snap, then came to sit down himself. They didn't look at each other as the plane began to make its descent and the silence between them was sharp enough to cut glass.

His hand still made that possessive anchor to her spine, though, when they left the plane, and the tense little quiver still made its strike down her front.

Formalities were swift and efficient. The night air was hot and heavy with the seductive aroma of spice. The car was a sturdy four-wheel drive with plenty of room to stack their luggage in the boot. And their driver, Santo, greeted them with a set of wonderful white teeth and the kind of warmth Lizzy didn't think she was ever going to feel penetrate to her bones again.

'I thought you said there would only be pelicans here,' she said as they skirted above what looked like a pretty town clustered around a horseshoe-shaped harbour where she could see the yachts swaying gently in the moon-washed night.

Luc didn't answer for a moment—long enough to inch up the tension between them some more. Then, 'I was being sardonic.'

It was death to any vague hope Lizzy might have had that they could return to some kind of normality after the ugly scene on the plane. Pressing her lips together, she said nothing else, just stared at the shadowy shapes of an alien landscape sweeping past her window. It was only as they turned in through a pair of gates and she saw a beautiful sugar-pink plantation house standing in front of them that she suddenly wondered if this was where he'd meant to bring Bianca too.

Then—*Don't!* she told herself angrily. Stop playing this pathetic torment with yourself. Aren't things bad enough as they are?

A swarm of staff came out to meet the vehicle. Doors were opened for them, the still heat of the night became filled with warm smiles and even warmer congratulations that included hugs and happiness on their behalf until Luc gave the order for it to stop.

The house itself looked as if it had been transported here right off the set of a period movie. Lizzy could almost see the ladies in crinolines gliding out onto the front porch.

She could hear and smell the ocean though she couldn't see it, and the heavy scent of tropical jasmine hung like a drug in the air.

'Come,' Luc said, making another one of those small hesitations, then rested an arm about her shoulders—for the comfort of the staff, Lizzy realised, and didn't push him away.

But those hesitations were beginning to speak volumes. He didn't want to touch her. Her silly confession about her lack of sexual experience had given him the biggest turn-off of his life. Now a wall was up and the detached cool was back, and it showed in the way he walked and the way he spoke so smoothly and quietly to the milling staff.

Inside the house was just as beautiful as his Lake Como villa, but decorated differently in cool pastel shades.

Lizzy stepped away from him as soon as she dared to, to glance around the huge open hallway with a white marble staircase sweeping upwards to a galleried first floor. A huge fan hung from the ceiling gently humming away and disturbing her hair as she spun slowly on the heels of her shoes.

'We will do the proper introductions tomorrow, but this is Nina, *cara*...'

Swinging to face Luc, she found him standing with his eyes carefully hooded and his face like a blank golden space. Her own eyes flickered slightly as she moved them sideways to where a tiny creature with beautiful dark brown skin stood smiling shyly at her.

'Nina manages the house and the staff,' Luc's carefully modulated voice explained, 'so if you need anything go to her.'

Finding a smile from somewhere, Lizzy stepped up to say hello and to offer Nina her hand.

'I am very happy to see you here, Signora De Santis,' Nina returned with a smiling formality that made Lizzy feel like a fraud. 'May I offer you both our delighted congratulations on behalf of all the staff here?'

Considering the rush of congratulations they'd just received outside, Nina's carefully rehearsed speech kind of fell flat. Still Lizzy managed an adequate reply while sensing the tension that hit the man standing at her side.

'My wife will want to go upstairs to—freshen up and

change,' he said calmly, with the 'my wife' sounding hollow to Lizzy's sensitised ears.

'I will show you, *signora*,' Nina said. 'Please,' she invited, 'this way…'

Lizzy walked in Nina's wake, aware that Luc remained standing where he was watching her. She was halfway up the stairs when she heard his footsteps echo off the tiled floor, but refused to look down and check where he'd gone.

The bedroom suite was beautiful, a soothing melody of pale blues and ivory and soft eau-de-Nil. Two maids were busy unpacking their bags for them. Another fan spun quietly above a huge mahogany four-poster bed, and yet another one hummed across the room above the French windows in front of which a table and two chairs stood, already set for two.

'There is a bathroom, *signora*, through here,' Nina was saying, pulling Lizzy's attention to the door she was holding open to reveal soft gold and cream tones of Italian marble. 'Would you like one of the maids to draw you a bath?'

'Oh, n-no—thank you,' Lizzy murmured shyly. 'I think I'll just—explore first if that's okay.'

'Of course. You want to settle in.' Nina nodded, let go of the bathroom door, then clapped her hands at the two hovering maids. 'Come, both of you, we will leave the new *signora* to catch her breath.'

Well, that was one way of putting it, Lizzy supposed as she kept her smile fixed until all three had left the room.

Then she wilted like a dying flower into a chair, shoulders sinking, face paling, eyes feeling suddenly very empty as she stared at the huge four-poster bed with its drapes of fine white silk.

One huge bed, two large dark mahogany wardrobes—her

gaze drifted over to them next—and two sets of fancy luggage standing half unpacked in front of each. One large very classy bathroom—from what she'd glimpsed through the gap when Nina had held the door open—and a table set for two by the window with a single red hibiscus flower standing in a tiny white vase, and two ivory-white candles floating in frosted glass bowls of water, just waiting to be lit.

Plus one wilting bride sitting here and a reluctant groom out there somewhere, probably downing brandy by the glassful while grimly ruing his lot.

The perfect honeymoon in paradise.

Getting up, she walked over to the suitcases to check which set belonged to her. She recognised nothing either in the cases or from what was hanging already in the wardrobe. She was a bought bride with just about every detail of her old life stripped away from her—except for the one thing he didn't want to have and wished weren't there at all.

Bending down, she flicked through a stack of soft designer lingerie. Sexy, every single set—purchased to seduce—plus bikinis in different styles and colours but no modest one-piece. Then there were the clothes that shrieked designer at her— bright, modern, chic and sassy to reflect current fashion trends.

Great.

Sighing, she turned and headed for the bathroom, then stood looking around it. One wickedly decadent deep plunge bath with optional whirlpool, two big shower cubicles, one toilet bowl and two white porcelain basins standing side by side above which hung mirrors and several glass shelves filled with bottles and tubes and jars of every beauty aid a woman could wish for.

And she refused—absolutely—to let herself question if all of this had been meant for Bianca.

Instead she stripped off, picked a shower cubicle and stepped into it.

Ten minutes later she walked back into the bedroom, wryly unsurprised to find that the maids had been in and finished the unpacking while she'd been showering.

Wrapped in one of the towelling bathrobes she'd found hanging behind the door, she rubbed at her wet hair with a towel as she wandered over to the window to look out. On impulse she tried the handle and found that the window was unlocked. Pushing it open showed her a bleach-boarded veranda with white slatted rails. The wood was warm beneath her bare feet as she stepped onto it, the heat of the night kind of soothing, and she stood leaning lightly against the rail and rubbing her hair while she tried to make out what the view in front of her was like.

It was truly pitch-dark out there but she caught the frothing white roll of a wave as it came into shore. It wasn't far away, perhaps a few hundred yards at most. And as her eyes grew more used to the darkness she managed to make out the shape of a white-painted gazebo not far from the beach.

It was then as she strained to focus on it that she captured a brief glimpse of Luc's face. He was standing beside the gazebo, nothing more than a shadowy bulk.

'You will get bitten by mosquitoes if you stay out here for much longer,' his cool voice drifted up to her.

'Don't be such a spoilsport or I'll go and find myself a large bottle of brandy and enjoy myself.'

He laughed; it was deep and sardonic. 'I might join you.'

This was crazy. Lizzy sighed. 'Is all of this macho sulking because I've spoiled your honeymoon plans?' she demanded. 'Because if it is I hope you are enjoying yourself!'

With that she turned and walked back into the bedroom closing the window with an angry click.

He arrived through the bedroom door as she was fastening her damp hair back with pins. Pushing a wide shoulder against the door frame, he slid his hands into his trouser pockets.

Tall, dark, handsome—sexy. Lizzy wanted to take her eyes off him but the flair that was happening in the pit of her stomach was stopping her from looking away.

'Do we try to bring this crazy marriage back on track or do we crack open the brandy bottle?' he asked in a cynical mocking kind of voice.

'Crazy just about says it.' Lizzy shrugged, turning away so she could put down her comb. 'I think the only reason we made it this far was because we hardly made contact during last week.'

'Hell of a week for me, *cara*. I was juggling weddings and brides and fathers-in-law and the media.'

'Thank God for pre-prepared honeymoons in paradise, then.'

It was out before she could stop it, but it wasn't just what she said but the way that she said it that made her go still with her shoulders slumping wearily, and made him as silent as the grave.

'This isn't going to work,' she whispered shakily. 'I think I want to go h-home.'

'To your unforgiving father?'

Oh, that was just deliberately cruel! Lizzy winced. He released a heavy sigh.

'Bianca wanted to visit her relatives in Australia so we were going to spend our honeymoon living out of a hotel that overlooked the opera house,' he informed her flatly. 'She would not have liked it here—too quiet, and there is nowhere for her to show off and shine. I'm surprised she didn't tell you all about her Sydney plans, since she informed me that she tells you everything.'

'As we both now know, Bianca didn't always tell the truth,' Lizzy murmured, referring to the huge act her friend had put on while planning to run away with Matthew. 'I'm—sorry,' she said then, 'for constantly jumping to the wrong conclusions.'

Luc just grimaced, as sombre as hell now. 'Nina has prepared us a light supper. Would you prefer to eat here or downstairs?'

End of subject, Lizzy recognised, her gaze drifting over to the romantic table set for two. 'Downstairs I think,' she said as she looked back at him.

He just nodded and straightened up from the door. 'Five minutes, then,' and he walked away—and if he glanced at the table by the window, Lizzy didn't see him do it.

Five minutes later she walked down the stairs to find Nina waiting for her. 'Signor Luc is in the small dining room, *signora*,' she said. 'I will show you the way.'

He was sitting at a round dining table idly pinching prawns from a steaming bowl of pasta while he waited for her to arrive. Another red hibiscus flower stood in a tiny white vase in the centre of the table and the candlelight came from several sources, flickering across the white tablecloth and against fine crystal wineglasses and his lean dark face.

He came to his feet when he saw her hovering in the doorway, his golden eyes shadowing over as he scanned them down the short dusky mauve empire-line dress she'd decided to wear. Nerve-ends fluttered in response to his sombre scrutiny, and Lizzy hated the self-conscious bloom she felt warm her cheeks.

It didn't help that everything about him was so sense-crushingly elegant. Somehow in the last five minutes he'd managed to change into a white shirt left open at his throat and a pair of black silk trousers that accentuated the powerful length of his legs.

'Pre-planning,' he said, using her word from earlier with a dry cut to his voice.

'I wish you would stop reading my mind,' Lizzy complained as she walked forward.

'Your face is—expressive.'

Oh, I really needed to know that, Lizzy thought helplessly and muttered a husky thanks when he politely held her chair for her.

'I know you are probably not hungry,' he said in a lighter voice as he returned to his own seat. 'But try to eat some of this for Nina's sake. I think she's confused enough about what's going on between us, without us offending her by rejecting her food.'

Lizzy nodded. She had seen the anxious expression on the housekeeper's face when she'd come down the stairs. For a honeymoon couple supposedly so wildly in love with each other they'd been willing to take on the censure of the world just to be together, the way they were behaving had to look strange.

So, on a deep breath that pulled in a bit shaky, she reached out for the bowl of pasta and spooned a few helpings onto his plate, then did the same for her own. Luc produced a bottle of champagne from an ice bucket set by his chair and popped the cork.

'More pre-planning?' Lizzy mocked.

He just sent her a brief smile as he poured frothing foam

into two crystal flutes. 'You don't touch this until you have eaten some pasta,' he instructed.

Lizzy uttered a small laugh. 'You sound like my father.'

He stiffened. 'That was not my intention.'

Staring at the carved lines on his face, she realised that she'd touched that raw nerve again in this man with nerves made of steel.

He didn't like to be compared with her father, she realized. It offended him. Nor did he always recognise a tease.

And he didn't like virgins.

The supper continued in near silence after that, his withdrawal from the sparring arena as obvious as the stern expression he wore on his face. And Lizzy had killed her own chances of managing light conversation when she'd let herself remember what was supposed to come next.

Her main problem being—she didn't know what came next. She'd known on the flight over here. For the whole week before the flight over here she'd known exactly what was going to come next because Luc had spelt it out to her in cool, precise language.

Marriage, sex, babies—little De Santis cubs.

'It's late.' She stood up, with no idea why she picked that precise moment to throw in the keeping-up-appearances towel. 'I think I'll—go to bed.'

She didn't look at him, but she could feel his eyes on her, feel his sombre mood. And he didn't say anything, just sat there lounging in his seat twisting a champagne flute between his fingers as he watched her make her retreat.

The pale blue curtains had been drawn across the window and the intimate table for two had been cleared. The bed had been turned down and the lights in the room had been reduced to a misty glow either side of the bed. As she stared at the bed Lizzy hugged herself and shivered as if she were standing in the coldest place on earth.

Slipping out of her clothes and into the smoothest white silk nightdress she'd ever run her fingers over, she tugged pins out of her hair until her scalp stung with the angry, frustrated violence she used.

She didn't look in a mirror—she didn't want to see what was written on her face. She just crawled between the cool linen sheets, punched the pillow with a clenched fist, then laid her head on it and willed herself to go to sleep.

It took hours—hours of lying there willing and wishing, and replaying the events of the day through a revolving door of spinning images and arguments and...waiting. At some point she must have accepted that her wedding night was going to be the same sterile event her wedding day had been because she finally managed to relax and drop into a deep, dark sleep.

She was warm and relaxed and beautifully comfortable dreaming about gentle waves rolling into a soft sandy shore, when the feel of a set of long fingers gently massaging the silk covering her stomach brought her awake.

She opened her eyes, felt the lazy moist warmth of a pair of lips taste the sensitive hollow by her ear—and tensed.

CHAPTER SEVEN

'NO, BE STILL,' Luc's dark husky voice commanded.

But the vibrating rush of sensual panic made Lizzy's heart beat a fast tattoo against her ribs and on a soft breath she flipped onto her back, eyes wide and staring up at him through the darkness.

'I thought you—'

He kissed the words away, sealing his lips to her lips and gently teasing the tiny tremor with his tongue. 'We are going to rescue our wedding night, *amore*,' he told her, 'and we will take it very slowly, so slowly you will not remember to be scared.'

Lizzy wanted to say that she wasn't scared but she couldn't, the hand at her stomach awakening her senses to the message being relayed to them by the slow, sensual caress his fingers made across the slippery silk. And she could feel the heat of him as he leant over her, feel that the full length of his body pressing intimately against hers was naked and aroused.

She closed her eyes and parted her lips for him, felt his sigh as he took the invitation and sank his tongue into her mouth, gently at first, then with deepening passion as she responded, catching the increasingly erotic rhythm of his tongue stroking against hers. Her hands lifted up to clutch at him, her finger-nails digging into the muscles braced like stretched satin in his arms, her body arching upwards in a compulsive need to press against that massaging hand.

As if the telling movement triggered something inside him, he slid the hand lower, skimming over her hips and her thighs to reach for the edge of her nightgown, then with a smooth, swift, experienced efficiency stripped it all the way up to her throat.

The loss of his mouth and the slick, lithe way he removed the scrap of silk over her head set her shivering and gasping, then the kiss was deep and hungry again, the massaging hand gliding now, over her newly exposed flesh. He stroked her thighs, the gentle contours of her hip and the indentation of her waist. When she whispered something into his mouth, he rose up and looked down her length to watch as his fingers moved on over the flat of her stomach to skim across the top of one pale rounded breast.

Lizzy closed her eyes when she felt the possessive claim that hand made and was ready this time for the burning wave of pleasure that drenched her as he stroked, then cupped, then grazed the aching tip with the pad of his thumb. Her nipples sprang out in a blatant leap and she squirmed in embarrassment.

He wasn't embarrassed. He just used his long fingers to shape the quivering globe in preparation to take that tight dark rosebud into his mouth. A piercing hot sting struck from the centre of her nipple and shot all the way down to her thighs, bending her body like a wand. Once again he lifted his dark head and looked at her, then strung a gentle line of slow, tender kisses along the line of her jaw. Lizzy closed her eyes and endured until at last he stopped teasing and gave her what she wanted—the warm, seductive pressure of his mouth on her own.

She kissed him as if she would die if she didn't. She floated on a sexual high. When he tried to calm her, she ran her fingernails into his hair and scored them down his back.

'Il virago inglese,' he accused on a rough shaken shudder.

Lizzy didn't care. She wanted his touch, she wanted to toss herself back to where they'd been on that other bed, before she'd chickened out and called a stop. And she wanted to feel every sensual sensation she knew was still waiting for her to experience.

So the tense curse that left his chest meant nothing to her until he used the superior strength in his arms to bring her tumbling halfway back down to earth.

'I said slowly,' he husked at her. 'I will not ravish you, Elizabeth.'

But she didn't know the difference between fast and slow. Her own wild senses were ruling her actions; the sweet, tight pulse of desire was controlling the pace. The fingers she sent spearing into his neck so she could bring his mouth back to hers were fierce and urgent. 'I want to be ravished,' she whispered to him.

His kiss-heated lips twisted into a grim smile. 'You don't understand the concept and I will not give you an excuse to accuse me of ravishing you once it is done and your conscience decides to torment you.'

Her eyes widened in protest. 'I w-wouldn't do that—'

'You would,' he insisted. 'You want me but you don't want to want me, you have simply allowed yourself to forget that. In fact,' he added, sending a sardonic gleam to her liquid green eyes, 'I predict you will take great pleasure in accusing me of anything that might come to mind.'

'How can you be so cold and detached that your mind

can even think of these things right now?' she threw at him helplessly.

'I am not cold and detached.' But his dark face clenched. 'I am just trying to play this as fairly as I can for you!'

'Me?' Lizzy choked out a laugh, feeling the whole wretched, glorious wash of pleasure swirl into bitterness. 'You haven't been fair to me since you met me.' Clenching her fists, she used them to try and push him away. 'You're a lousy lover, Luc,' she added in thick frustration when she couldn't budge him by even half an inch. 'The kind that sounds like he wants me to sign another contract before he condescends to move this marriage on!'

Once again her tongue had outpaced her common sense. Lizzy knew it the moment the cutting accusation was out. Her breathing disappeared, her eyelashes flickering as she took in the look that had frozen his face. Teeth burying themselves into her full bottom lip, she waited, heart pounding, her foolish stubbornness refusing to let her take the words back before it was too late.

And she knew she should have done—his complete stillness told her that she should. Yet he didn't move, didn't speak, he didn't make any really visible sign that she'd managed to cut into him at all. It was just there in the pulsating silence, in the way she was suddenly feeling the difference in their age and experience, and in the tiny quivers stinging her muscles in places they should not be doing at a tense moment like this.

'S-say something,' she breathed when she could stand it no longer.

He moved then, like a man who had just come to a grim decision. One of his arms snaked outwards and suddenly a light switched on, bathing them both in a soft golden glow that did nothing to lessen Lizzy's tension one bit. She actually felt her eyes turn black. Yet he still just continued to look down at her, into her huge wary eyes and the silken tumble of chestnut curls rippling the pillow around her delicately featured very pale face.

And her heart wasn't beating fast now, it was thumping slow and thick. His face, his beautiful, beautiful face was still so expressionless it just didn't go with what he did next.

What he did was to spear his long fingers into her hair, then curve them around the back of her neck. As she gasped he tilted her head back so it arched her slender white throat, then lowered his dark head and buried his mouth in her taut, smooth flesh.

Nothing in her meagre experience with men helped to warn her as to what was coming. It was seduction at its most deep and determined level. It was the man of experience making no concessions for her foolishly defiant innocence. He made love to her with a grim and silent precision; he dragged each and every sensually erotic sensation to the stinging surface of her pale, smooth, receptive skin. He moved his mouth in hot, sensual glides until he reached her parted, trembling mouth, then he kissed her long and deep and without mercy until she was dizzy with it, throbbing and drunk. And he used his hands and his mouth and his tongue in ways and in places she hadn't known could be so deliciously good.

The quiet command of his voice worked her like a puppet. She was trapped, enslaved by the string-pulling power of his knowledge and her own desire to feel whatever he decided to bestow on her too-responsive flesh. He caressed each curve and hollow and soft warm crevice of her body; he drew her taut with exquisite sensation with his hands and his mouth and his teeth. He kneaded the rounded, swollen fullness of her breasts and sent her teeth into his satin, taut shoulder when he teased and sucked their eager tips.

She even felt him tremble once or twice when her restless, untutored fingers scraped across his flesh. And when the downward glide of his trailing fingers finally took control of the pulsing ache between her legs she flailed in a morass of hot feeling, lost to reality because her own heady consciousness had locked onto the will of her body and the way he slowly, relentlessly brought her climbing and crawling and panting and needing to a whimpering, pleading peak.

No single part of her did not know what it was like to be caressed by him—no nerve-end, no muscle, no velvet dark place of intimacy, until she pulsed and throbbed and breathed out his name in a helpless, breathless, sensual chant.

She hadn't opened her eyes in ages, not since she'd lowered her eyelids in surrender and let him do this to her. But as she felt his weight easing down on top of her and her thighs being urged apart her eyelids lifted, her eyes making deep, deep contact with the heavy gold darkness in his.

Everything about him was heavy gold darkness, the breadth of his shoulders blocking out most of the lamplight, the long, hard-muscled torso pressing down on her with his hips. She felt the presence and the power of his erection nudge against her carefully prepared warm and wet and swollen flesh. His mouth was still somber, but it was tender when he took her mouth in yet another deep, drugging kiss.

Then it was there. His hands cupped her bottom to lift her and he made that first smooth, blinding thrust with his hips.

Her body throbbed and stretched to accommodate him; she
felt him like a burning shaft of fire in the innocence of her
sheath. Her breath caught, her fingers dug into his shoulders
and sensation poured in a swirling wave of fear and anticipation down the pulsing length of where they had joined.

'You are sure you want this?' he husked at her.

The fact that he'd even asked the question after so much
pulsing macho male domination made tears sting the back of
her throat. The point surely was—did *he* want it?

Lizzy nodded, her mouth just a breath away from his
mouth, her eyes clinging dark and vulnerable and helplessly
needy to his. It was his eyes that closed when he made that
final invasion, his mouth that quivered tautly as she tried to
choke back a cry of pain. It was his hands that trembled as
he pushed the hair away from her face, then kissed it, kissed
it in soft, soothing touches until he felt the tension slowly seep
out of her. Then she felt him go deeper, felt the singing dance
of her nerve-ends clamour to his probing force. His hands
were gliding down the silken thighs to her calves then, and
lifting them until her legs circled his waist.

The action sent him even deeper, he shuddered and whispered something in Italian she did not catch, then he was
folding her into the strong embrace of his arms and moving—
moving, feeding them both into a sensuously searing rhythm
that throbbed like a living entity inside her. Her fingers clung
to his back as he increased the pace with each hot, pleasur-
able thrust. She knew where she was going but didn't know
how to reach it. She whimpered anxiously against his mouth.

He caught hold of her hair again to push her head backwards. 'Look at me,' he said, and she lifted heavy eyelids she
hadn't been aware of closing, to be trapped in the burning

dark flames in his eyes. Then, like that, he made it happen
for her, made her body quicken and finally surrender to the
bright and sizzling accelerated rush.

Her first cry broke his rhythm from deep and slow to short
and fast and she lost it—lost whatever it was she'd been desperately hanging onto as she shot on an explosion of fierce
pleasure into wild white pulsating light, while he held her and
watched her and orchestrated each wave as it battered into
her, each helpless cry, each quivering, broken, convulsive
tremor that just seemed to go on and on and on…until with
a low, thick groan he joined her, spilling heat on the flames
with a sharp stabbing movement that sent an ecstatic pleasure
rippling through every muscle and bone and sinew he had.

Seduction, she acknowledged long minutes later when she
finally drifted back to earth again. I've just been completely,
beautifully, thoroughly and ruthlessly seduced.

He still hadn't moved and his weight was heavy on her;
she could feel the still-pounding beat of his heart against her
crushed breasts. She became aware that her legs were still
wrapped around him, though their bodies were no longer intimately joined.

Still, she knew the image of the two of them like this was
going to live with her for the rest of her life.

Coupling, she named it.

It was that physical and basic.

Releasing the still trembling tension out of her limbs, she
slid them away from him. As if her movement made him also
decide to move, he levered himself up onto a forearm, reached
out and switched off the light.

It was so abrupt, so stunningly final. He didn't release her
when he shifted his weight onto the bed beside her, but there

were no words spoken between them, no clash of eyes. It was as if now it was over he was expecting them both to just fall asleep.

It hurt. It made vulnerable tears sting the backs of her eyes and her throat. She was damp between her legs and the lingering tremor of pleasure still worked within her as her stretched muscles slowly contracted back to their original state.

When she couldn't bear it and tried to speak he just put his hand to the back of her head and pressed her face into the prickly dark warmth of his chest.

He fell asleep like that—holding her. Lizzy had never felt so wretched in her entire life. Had she brought it on herself? Was this grim silent aftermath her reward for persistently taking stabs at him—at his irritatingly unflappable control, at his prowess as a lover? She wished she knew why she did it. She wished she understood how she could resent him so angrily yet want him so badly. She just didn't understand herself at all.

She tried to move away from him, but his powerful arms held her fast. Oddly—again—she found she liked being held by him and slowly let her muscles relax.

It didn't occur to her that he was lying there with his eyes wide open, and that each time she moved against him he was having to fight to keep his response in check.

And she didn't know that while she was seeing what they'd just done as a basic coupling, he was seeing it as the most soul-stripping experience of his cynical sexual life.

Lizzy drifted asleep in the warm cocoon of his arms and awoke late the next morning to find an empty place beside her in the bed. In a way it was a relief. No awkward moments having to face him while her defences were down, no stumbling around trying to think of something to say that wouldn't come out sounding silly and vulnerable and gauche. She could shower at her leisure and get her act together.

No, she couldn't. Instead she sank down on the edge of the plunge bath and let the whole high octane event of her wedding night rush through her head and her body in small explosions of remembered feelings, few of which made her feel good about herself—or about him.

What were they doing to each other? *Why* were they doing it? All Lizzy knew as she sat there remembering the hot tempo of their passionate coupling was that somehow, in the last week leading up to last night, she had allowed Luc De Santis to become a terrible fever of desire that had built and built inside her until it had taken her over.

Because she loved him—?

No! She stood up with a jerk. *No*, she didn't love him. She didn't *want* to love him!

Dear God, don't let me go down that no-hope route.

Coming down the stairs half an hour later took courage because she still hadn't reconciled last night in her head. And she ached all over, in places she didn't think it was possible to ache, places that made her feel sensitive and self-aware and—yes, scared of what to expect from him when they met.

Unsure where to go once she reached the hallway, she followed her instincts and found herself back in the room they'd eaten supper in the night before. It was late, almost lunchtime by her reckoning, though her body clock was so up the creek, she wasn't sure if that meant lunchtime in Italy or lunchtime here because she'd forgotten to put on her watch when she'd changed before she'd left the Lake Como villa.

The room looked different in the daylight. Bigger and

bright, with the sun shaded from streaming in through the wide open windows by a huge striped awning she could see rippling softly in the breeze outside. Beneath it was a smooth stone patio stretching out to the glinting blue of a large swimming pool, and beyond that the lush colourful growth of a lovingly tended tropical garden leading right down to the edge of a blinding white sandy beach, then the rich turquoise-blue of the Caribbean sea. No sign of the gazebo from this side of the house, she noticed, and the waves that washed the shore lapped gently as if they were too lazy to foam and roll.

A sound from behind her made her turn sharply, expecting to find Luc, only to watch Nina come hurrying into the room with a beaming smile on her face.

'Ah, so you have surfaced, *signora*. Mr Luc said to leave you to sleep your jet lag away, but I was beginning to worry that you would never wake up to this beautiful, beautiful day!'

The housekeeper's gushing bright chatter eased some of the tension out of Lizzy's body. Within minutes she was sitting in the same chair she'd sat in the night before, sipping freshly squeezed orange juice and eating slices of delicious fresh fruit with Nina still fussing around her like a mother hen taking care of a brand-new chick.

'Please call me Lizzy,' she said after the *signora* began to grate. She didn't feel like a *signora*, she didn't even feel like *Mrs*, though the gold ring on her finger told her she was.

Which then asked the question—what did she feel like?

'Mr Luc went out after his breakfast to check on his farmers, as he always does when he arrives here,' Nina was saying, gaining Lizzy's attention quicker than anything else could.

'His farmers?' she prompted.

Nina gave a nod, pouring steaming coffee into her coffee-cup. 'He didn't tell you? This house and the land belonged to his grandmamma. Her portrait hangs in the main salon. I will show you later, if you like. Mr Luc spent a lot of his childhood here, during the school holidays. His grandmother was a forceful lady who pioneered the concept of collective farming on the island. Mr Luc has continued her success in the wake of her untimely death last year.'

Last year? Lizzy had not known that Luc had suffered such a loss so recently.

Nina nodded. 'We still miss her—Mr Luc most of all. She made him human, he once told me.' The housekeeper paused to offer up a sigh. 'It is the downside of being born into great wealth and responsibility, I suppose, that you switch off your softer instincts so you will keep yourself strong.' Then she showed Lizzy her wonderful smile again. 'Now you are here to make him feel human, heh?' The gleam in her rich brown eyes made Lizzy burn. 'His grandmamma would like you. You have a look of her, and you are stubborn like she was, and—'

'English,' a different voice drawled.

Lizzy froze in the process of picking up a juicy chunk of fresh pineapple, her eyes skittering towards the door where he stood leaning against the framework, casual as hell dressed in pale chinos and a blue tee shirt, his hair ruffled as if by the breeze. Every inch of him was long, lithe, so spare of flesh it was like looking at a breathtaking study of firm-muscled, lean golden strength that set her senses responding with tight little pulses deep down in the intimate place between her legs.

'Virago.' The housekeeper turned to smile at him, seemingly unaware as to how the tension in the room had just rocketed. 'You called her the English virago.'

'*Il virago inglese,*' he softly translated, then watched, his eyes mostly hidden beneath the heavy fall of his soot-black eyelashes, the telling dark flush march up Lizzy's throat and cheeks.

He'd called her that last night, when she'd buried her teeth in him. He'd said something similar to her on the plane. Stifled beyond speech by the endearment's link with one of his close family, she dropped the piece of pineapple back onto the plate and came jerkily to her feet.

'*Buon giorno, la mia moglie bella,*' he murmured smoothly then, the hidden gold in his eyes flaring briefly as they took in her tiny white vest-top and her short blue skirt.

Lizzy was suddenly excruciatingly aware of the pinprick sting of her nipples inside the flimsy white cups of her bra, and the amount of leg left on show by the shortness of the skirt. Her hair was tied back and she wished that it weren't as a fresh layer of heat seeped into her cheeks. She wished she were standing here in a full-length woollen coat despite the overwhelming Caribbean heat.

'No reply for me, *cara*?' he mocked her numbing silence.

No, she thought, because I just can't speak yet. Instead she used her tongue to soothe the sudden tremor that had developed across her lips. He watched it happen, and there was nothing on his face to tell her what he was thinking, yet she sensed a tension in him that literally picked at her flesh as he dipped those eyes down her full length once again.

'So my sweet virgin bride is robbed of speech,' he mocked her. 'Perhaps there is some hope left for my lousy technique.'

Lizzy tensed. '*Don't,*' she shivered out, mortified beyond bearing that he could say something like to her at all after last night and especially in front of his housekeeper.

'We are alone.' He smiled briefly at the way she flicked her startled eyes to the place where Nina had been standing. 'She beat a hasty retreat when you blushed so charmingly. And it is too late to keep your virgin status on our wedding night a secret, *amore*. There was blood on the sheets.'

The shockingly abrupt announcement froze the colour out of Lizzy's face.

'You did not notice?' Levering himself away from the door, he started moving towards her. 'One of the maids surely will have done when she remade the bed after you left it.'

Lizzy flinched when the sleeve to his shirt brushed her arm as he reached past her to pick up her discarded piece of pineapple.

'No comment,' he mocked when she still said nothing. 'I admit, when I saw it, it made me feel positively medieval.' He put the pineapple into his mouth. 'I half expected to arrive back here this lunchtime to see the evidence hanging from the window as proof of your chastity and my undoubtedly—'

With a stifled choke, Lizzy turned and ran, switching the cruel battery of his words off like a flick of a switch. As she made it into the hall without throwing up she wondered bitterly if the heavy crash she heard behind her was a sign that he was angry he'd been left mocking a lost audience!

Outside the heat was so intense she almost changed her mind and went back into the coolness of the house. But—no. Burning alive was a better option than going back in there, she thought painfully as she took off across the grass, heading for—she didn't know where or care.

She did not understand what made him want to be so constantly cruel to her. Twenty-four hours as his bought bride and already she did not know how much more of it she could take.

Dropping down on the stone steps of the gazebo, she hugged her knees to her chest and stared out to sea. She was trembling, her mind filled with lurid images of giggling maids whispering their secret to the rest of the staff here. Luc had called it medieval, Lizzy wanted to call it—

A step sounded close beside her, shutting off her painful thought patterns to replace them with a whole aching set of new ones.

CHAPTER EIGHT

'I'M—SORRY,' Luc murmured tautly. 'That was unforgivably brutal of me.'

So he was aware of it? Lizzy supposed it had to mean something at least. Though thinking that did not stop the glaze of hurt from washing across her eyes before she blinked it away again.

'When you've had enough of punishing me for being the wrong woman you married,' she whispered, 'do me one small favour, Luc, and arrange my flight home for me, please.'

His sigh was carried away on the light breeze coming in from the ocean. When he dropped down into a squat in front of her and gently touched his fingers to her pale cheek, she refused to look at him and still just wanted to break down and weep.

'I was shocked,' he said gruffly, 'when I saw the— evidence myself this morning. I felt I had stolen something from you that did not belong to me.'

'That's your only excuse?' Lizzy still would not look at him.

'No. I have others,' he admitted, 'though I don't think you're ready to hear them right now.'

He was probably right. She'd heard more than enough of

his cynical view of everything. Her heart was breaking into little pieces in her chest and her eyes were still stinging.

'I will not take the stick you should be beating Bianca with,' she told him thickly. 'You spoiled last night for me— twice, counting your performance just now—and I think you did it deliberately.'

'I attack when I am on the defensive.'

Doesn't everyone? Lizzy thought painfully.

'I expected you to throw some deserved accusations at me just now, so I got in first.'

'You know what you are, Luc?' At last she turned her face to look at him, and felt no sympathy whatsoever for the now penitent expression she saw on his handsome dark face. 'You're so cold and cynical about everything you don't recognise feelings in others. You believe you can treat me with contempt because I made it so obvious from the start that I'm—attracted to you.'

A strange smile touched his tense mouth. 'Not contempt,' he denied.

'So there was blood on the sheets,' Lizzy continued unsteadily. 'A sensitive man would have gently pointed it out to me, but not you. You stride off into the day without a care as to what the embarrassment was going to do to me.'

'I thought you would have noticed it for yourself.'

'Well, I didn't.' She turned away again. In truth she hadn't dared look at the bed once she'd scrambled out of it. 'And what is it you find so wrong with my—inexperience?' she challenged suddenly. 'Why do you believe it's okay to mock it, *make* a mockery of it?'

'I can do better.'

Too late for Lizzy.

'Yesterday I was—angry about a lot of things,' he disclosed. 'Things I should not have brought into our bedroom and should not have carried with me out of it this morning. Now I am asking you to accept my apology and my promise that I can and will do better from now on.'

Quite a speech for the sardonic man who believed himself above such things.

'You're hunting,' she murmured absently.

There was a sharp moment of shock, then the soft sound of rueful laughter, then his fingers returned to her cheek and firmly turned her face.

'I am hunting,' he agreed with a real smile that actually relaxed his tense features, 'which makes this a bad day for male lions, *cara*, because it means they must be feeling desperate.'

That was a message, Lizzy recognised, a serious hint wrapped up in a new kind of rueful warmth. She drew in a breath, wishing she could decide if this was just another one of his clever strategies aimed to keep his life running on its nice even keel.

'Make me feel ashamed of you once more,' she said finally, 'and I walk away from this marriage no matter what you threaten me with.'

To her surprise he just nodded, no clever quick counterattack, face still serious, the dark golden eyes wrapped in luxurious dark eyelashes, an even shape to his beautiful mouth. He'd dropped the cool mask, Lizzy realised, and all she was seeing now was the too handsome, worryingly alluring man.

Then he was rising to his full height and holding out a hand for her to take so he could help her up. Lizzy stared at that hand for a few seconds, still hesitant to take what she knew it was offering, yet too aware of the tingling sting of entice-ment at work in her blood to stop her own hand from lifting and settling into his. His fingers closed around hers and he drew her upright. When she tried to take her hand back he held onto it and used it to bring her even closer until she was standing a mere breath away from touch-close to his lean, hard, now very familiar length.

Her heart began to thump. He was going to kiss her, and she couldn't make up her mind if she wanted to be kissed right now. Tension inched up along the length of her spine and made the air shiver as it left her lungs.

'I n-need some things your wonderful style team forgot to pack in my luggage.' She went for a diversion on a quick agitated rush of speech.

'Like what?' he murmured.

The murmur was disturbingly husky. 'A gentleman doesn't ask that question,' she responded distractedly.

'I thought we had already established that I'm not one—a gentleman,' he added.

She looked up, at his mouth, saw the hint of a grimace taking control of it, felt her own lips tremble and part. 'A s-sunhat, then, and a truckload of sun screen,' she comprom-ised her answer, trying so hard not to sound as unnerved by his closeness as she actually felt.

But maybe he knew, maybe she even quivered. It was dif-ficult for her to tell any more because tense inner quivers around him had become such a permanent thing she was learning she had to live with. Anyway, he gave a tug at her hand. The thin gap between them disappeared altogether, the warmth of his body heat stimulated every nerve-end she pos-sessed and sent her eyes lifting up to clash warily with his.

Whatever he saw reflected in her eyes sent a strange kind of grimace moving across his lips. Then he did it—he kissed her.

It was such a brief embrace that it had gone before she could even think to react to it.

'Then let's go shopping,' was all he said.

Lizzy knew then that they had just sealed yet another deal between them, though heck if she had enough sense left to work out what this one was about.

And he was back to playing it cool again, being the guy who liked to be in control of everything—including his renegade wife. He drove them into town in a soft-top sports car with the roof firmly in place to keep the heat of the sun off her fair skin. They strolled in and out of small shops painted in different pretty pastel shades, each one carrying the kind of interestingly individual things that made Lizzy want to linger and browse.

He chose her sunhat while she wasn't looking, a wide, floppy-brimmed thing made of bright pink straw that he paid for, coolly put on her head, then walked her out of the shop without giving her the chance to object about the colour and the way it had to be clashing with the colour of her hair.

'Arrogant,' she muttered.

'All of my life,' he answered smoothly, and walked her into a pharmacy and proceeded to pick out the highest factor sun screen he could find and Lizzy let him because—

Well, why not? she told herself. He'd taken command of every other decision in her life, like her clothes, her wedding—her wedding night. So she left him to it and went off to find the other female-type items she'd wanted to buy that she'd left off her list back at the gazebo.

He paid the bill.

And she began to feel like a very mute, very pampered female with just enough resentment burning inside her to stop her from liking it.

As he walked beside her his hand was always in touch with her somewhere—her hand, her arm, the base of her spine—until they bumped into some people he knew, when his arm became that angled pressure across her back and the hand a long fingered clamp in the indentation of her waist that drew her in very close to his side.

Making a silent statement as he'd done at the wedding or being protective of his new bride? Lizzy didn't know but she leant into him anyway for protection as he introduced her as, 'My wife, Elizabeth.'

She could tell from their expressions that the news about their scandalous marriage had even reached as far as this tiny island in the Caribbean.

'*Cara*, this is Elena and Fabio Romano, friends of mine,' he completed the introductions.

Elena Romano was young and slender and extremely beautiful, but she wore the kind of curious gleam in her dark eyes that made Lizzy think of a black-eyed witch with long sharp nails. Fabio Romano was tall and tanned and middle-aged with a languid boredom about him that had her wondering if that was where Luc was going to be by the time he reached his middle years.

They said they were cruising the Caribbean on their yacht and invited Luc and Lizzy to join them for the afternoon. Luc was beautifully suave and gracious with his refusal. Fabio Romano was beautifully suave and gracious in his acceptance of it. His lovely wife was not. Her black eyes sparked with irritation, which she vented on Lizzy.

'Such a sweet hat, *cara*,' she murmured, 'very cute and—pink. How do you dare to wear that shade with your hair colouring?'

'Luc chose it,' Lizzy answered smoothly. 'He likes cute and pink.'

Elena's light laugh tinkled off into the sunlight. Lizzy felt the press of Luc's fingers as they bit into her waist.

'Ah,' Elena hadn't finished, 'that explains your wedding photograph in this morning's papers—' she nodded '—and the positively dramatic image you made of the pale young virginal bride standing next to her sternly reformed rake.'

Well, the cruelly perceptive bitch, Lizzy thought breathlessly. 'My style team managed to get it just right, don't you think?' She smiled through gritted white teeth.

She hadn't been around Bianca for years without learning how to respond to such a woman. And even if the floppy brim to her cute pink hat hadn't been blocking him off from the shoulders upwards, nothing on earth would have made her look up at him as she felt Luc's fingers bite into her again.

'And with so little notice.' Elena slid her eyes down to Lizzy's stomach, the suggestion she was implying shocking Lizzy into releasing a gasp.

'Gosh,' she rallied. 'It never entered my head that people would think poor Luc had been *forced* into marrying me!'

'They don't.' Surprisingly it was Fabio Romano who pulled himself out of his boredom to put a stop to this. 'Elena is fishing for information. She is always fishing for information—it is the staple diet for a professional bitch.'

Well, he said it, Lizzy's eyes told the other woman while Elena flushed. A few minutes later they'd made their polite farewells and were walking back to where they'd left the car.

'You were a great help,' Lizzy said, stiff with anger and a very bruised pride.

Luc, on the other hand, was coolly indifferent. 'You will learn soon enough that it is safer to say nothing at all around people like Elena.'

Well, Lizzy didn't want to learn to *be quiet*. If that was a brief taster of what was waiting for her when they returned to Italy, then she didn't want any part of it.

'She's attracted to you, which is why she got her nails into me.'

'Now you are being fantastical.'

'An ex-lover, then, with a grudge because she didn't end up your dramatically pale virginal bride.'

'You would have to go back a long way into Elena's past to find the virgin,' he laughed. 'And why are you angry with me when you were more than capable of handling the situation without any help from me?'

'I don't like your lifestyle,' she muttered.

He didn't say anything to that one. He just opened the car door for her and waited for her to get in. Lizzy pulled off her hat and placed it on her lap, then watched in simmering silence as he dropped her purchases at her feet before he shut her door and strode round the car bonnet to get in beside her.

'I want to see the photograph she was talking about,' she told him.

'No.' The engine vibrated beneath her on a low growling leap into life.

'Why not?' she persisted. 'Have you seen it?' she then demanded sharply.

All she got back was a view of his profile set in stone. Her head suddenly began to buzz as he swept them back up the hill towards the villa. Like little pieces of a jigsaw falling into place, Lizzy began to link that ugly scene he'd orchestrated this morning with what Elena Romano had said.

'You have seen it,' she declared in a hot, husky voice filled with fizzing resentment. 'It was the reason why you were so nasty to me this morning. You saw that photo and didn't like what it fed out there for everyone else to see—namely me, looking all pale and interesting, and you, looking like some poor rich guy who'd been caught by the oldest trick in the book.'

'You possess a wild imagination,' he drawled casually.

'I want to see it,' Lizzy repeated.

He said nothing, just pulled the car to a stop outside the sugar pink plantation house and climbed out of it. Lizzy did the same thing, glaring at him across the car's soft top. He was frowning, grimly ignoring her as if she were an irritating fly he would like to swat away with his hand.

Well, that was fine, she told herself as she stalked around the car and into the house. She wasn't a complete air-head. She knew a man like Luc didn't go anywhere unless he had a reliable connection to the internet.

So she began stalking the huge hallway, opening doors and glancing inside them before she moved on to the next.

'If you want to see over the whole house, *cara*,' his hateful voice murmured, 'I am happy to show you around without risking the paintwork on all the doors. Go away, Nina,' he added as a mere calm aside.

Lizzy turned in time to see the housekeeper disappearing towards the back of the house. *He* was standing in the middle of the pale marble floor looking so darn together against her sizzling anger that she wanted to fly at him with her nails un-sheathed.

Instead she balled her fingers into tense fists by her sides. 'If you and the rest of the world can see a picture of me at my own wedding, then *I* want to see it!' she insisted furiously.

'I assure you, you don't,' he said, smiled, then dropped the smile and shot out an impatient sigh when all she did was to spin her back to him and move on to fling open the next door. 'Why is it,' he snapped out, 'that everyone else gets to enjoy your placid side while I only get the—?'

His voice just stopped. Lizzy didn't notice. She was too busy taking in the room she had just stepped into filled with the softest light and gentle shadows—and a huge gold-framed portrait hanging from one of the pale blue walls.

'The virago,' she murmured, just too stunned to remember that she was supposed to be hunting down some kind of office in this many-roomed mansion. 'Dear God,' she added on a thick shaken swallow as her feet took her further into the room.

'La Contessa Alexandra De Santis,' Luc's deep dry voice fed to her from behind. 'Grande Dame, matriarch, bad mother, wonderful grandmother, and my other *virago inglese.*'

'She looks like me,' Lizzy whispered.

'I believe Nina said so,' he returned evenly.

'But you don't?' She was staring up at the face of a breath-takingly beautiful creature who could have come straight out of a Titian painting.

'Your hair is darker and your eyes are grey, not blue.'

But the shape of her mouth and the small pointed chin and the hourglass shape of her slender figure inside a gentian-blue gown that could only have been fashioned by the finest haute couture looked like Lizzy.

'How old is she here?' she asked on a reverent murmur.

'Forty nine,' he replied, dragging another gasp from Lizzy's shocked lips because she looked barely eighteen. 'My grandfather commissioned the painting as a gift for her fiftieth birthday. He claimed that her beauty was the only thing about her that kept them together. She claimed they stayed together because she allowed it, despite the countless affairs he enjoyed during their long marriage.'

'She loved him, you mean.'

'I like to think so, though I don't believe he deserved such devoted loyalty—and divorce was not heard of in Italian society in their day.'

'And she made him pay in other ways.'

'Now that was astute,' he said after a startled moment.

Because I feel like I know her outside and in, Lizzy thought breathlessly. And I'm standing right here with a man I wouldn't trust as far as I could pick him up and throw him.

'You think I am like my grandfather,' Luc murmured.

And *that* was astute of *him*. 'You take what you want,' she responded, 'because you believe you have a right to and you don't play fair while you do it.' Turning around, she pushed her chin up. 'I want to see that photograph now.'

His eyes took their time shifting from the portrait to the determined tilt of her face. What he was thinking didn't show. If he was still trying to compare her to his grandmother, it didn't show. If he had decided to marry her because she reminded him of probably the only person he had ever really loved, even that didn't show.

Hard, tough, unemotional, arrogant, she found herself listing all over again while she stood waiting for his response. The fact that she'd just realised he had a title attached to his name, though she'd never heard anyone use it, only added more reason as to why he was like he was.

Her heart began to thump oddly because he still wasn't saying anything and she was damned if she was going to back down now—even if there was something going on in those implacable golden eyes that she did not quite understand or like.

'We keep fighting,' he said finally.

Lizzy nodded, lips pinned together.

'And you persist in believing that you can win.'

Well, give up on that belief and she might as well lie down and let him trample all over her. 'I can use a computer, so if you just point me in the right direction...' she prompted.

He smiled. It wasn't a condescending smile, but neither was it pleasant. If she could see herself she'd probably be backing off, but she could not see how the defiant tilt of her chin was making her spiralling hair flame around her face or that the rounded shape of her breasts was moving too fast inside her top, nor was she aware that her nipples had sprung into two tantalisingly tight teasing buds.

He was aware, though, aware enough to allow his body to respond to temptation, aware enough to enjoy drawing out the tension between them until her eyelashes feathered down on her cheeks as she dropped her eyes from his.

She found her gaze settling on his throat. It was that taut golden throat that had been the cause of all her problems, she reminded herself. And the still vivid memory of her lips brushing against it made her suddenly burn to place her lips there again. It was a shock—her whole fascination with his throat was a bewildering puzzle she just could not understand. Yet it was there pulsing away with its bad temptation for her to just lean in and—

Maybe a retreat was sometimes a good idea, she heard herself think in a tense, anxious backtrack. 'I think I'll go and—'

'Coward.' He laughed softly—and moved so fast she didn't see it coming until she was already locked into his embrace and his mouth was hungry on hers.

It was a hot kiss, a long and demanding and seriously, seriously deep kind of kiss. When it was over she was breathless, the front of her body pressing into him with a soft and needy intimacy that brought a flush to her cheeks, and her only comfort was that she could feel the sense drenching evidence of his response pressing against her.

'I wish you would stop just grabbing me like this!' she managed to push out on a stifled whisper.

'I don't play fair,' he reminded her dryly, and captured her mouth again. By the time this one was over she was trembling against him and her fingers were clutching at the back of his neck.

'Fast or slow?' he husked, still toying sensually with the cushion soft heat of her mouth. 'Fast means we rip our clothes off and get very basic right here against the wall or down on the floor. Slow means we try to make it to the privacy of our bedroom. You choose.'

Choose? 'I don't know,' Lizzy mumbled helplessly. 'I'm not very good at all of this.'

'Trust me, *cara*, you are very good at it,' he responded harshly, though harsh in this case was very sexy.

So sexy she gave in to, and leant in to let her tongue make a half-clumsy slide on his taut golden skin. His rasping curse was exciting. The way his hands took hold of her by the waist and put her away from him brought a whispered, 'Sorry,' shaking from her lips.

He just grabbed hold of her hand and began trailing her behind him into the hallway, the decision apparently made for her as to where the rest of this was going to take place. He towed her up the stairs and into the bedroom. Shutting the door behind them, he then towed her over to the bed and propped her up against one of the posts.

'Don't move,' he said as he took a step back from her.

Lizzy only wished that she had the power to move, but she didn't. She just leant there and watched as he began to strip his clothes off. Dark olive skin wearing the gloss of warmth and the taut muscle formation that rippled as he moved was revealed to her in swift degrees. His tee shirt—gone, his long fingers dragging her eyes down the cluster-dark arrow of hair on his torso to watch, in churning anticipation, him unfasten his trousers and strip them away. He wore flat loafers that he heeled off and kicked to one side, no socks to cover his long brown feet. Only one item of clothing was left on his body, and her breathing grew piercingly tight as he stripped that away too.

'You like what you see?' he demanded silkily.

Lizzy glossed her lips with her tongue and nodded.

'You wish to lick me some more?'

'Yes, please,' she breathed.

He took that step back towards her, so impossibly beautiful and arrogant and powerful he made her heart pump deliriously.

'Enjoy,' he invited, and she couldn't believe how quickly she moved towards him, she couldn't believe it was she who was so eagerly touching him with her fingers, tasting him with her tongue and grazing his flesh with her teeth, while he stood there, passively allowing her with his hands grasping the bedpost so she was trapped in the circle of his arms.

Though he wasn't really passive—he flinched and flexed and breathed tautly to every move she made on him. When she stretched up for his mouth he gave it, when she bravely dared to run her fingers down through the mat of hair and explore the length of his erection, the velvet-smooth length jerked and pulsed.

And he was breathing as unevenly as she was, the tension in him clenching his muscles tight. When she flung her arms around his neck and just clung, he seemed to see it as some kind of surrender because he muttered something in Italian, then took control. Her skirt ripped because he couldn't be bothered to find the zip on it. As she gasped in shock it landed in a warm heap at her feet, and he was already bending down to strip away her panties. The hungry intrusion of his tongue between her legs before he straightened up again drew a keening cry from her throat. Her top went next, sliding over her head and disappearing out of her line of vision, her breasts bouncing as he released them from her bra. He caught them up in the cups of his long fingers, nothing prepared her for the hot wave of pleasure that danced through her as his mouth ravished their tender, tight peaks.

If this was slow in his estimation, it wasn't in Lizzy's. It was hot and passionately fast. Her fingers bit into the solid strength of his biceps, and she trembled and writhed, and kept her eyes closed because that way everything felt so much more powerful. When he finally tumbled her down onto the bed her slender legs parted so she could feel the full impact of him when he stretched himself out on top of her.

For a full sense-locking second she thought he was just going to take her right now like this, and she was shocked by how much she wanted him to. But he didn't. Slow came in an agony of new experiences; she was a physical, sensual, trembling wreck by the time he decided it was time.

And this was no coupling, she found herself thinking hazily as he came inside her with a long, slow, probing push that took the breath from her lungs. It was a hot, deep, passionate love-making where the two of them became one single unit moving and breathing and finally reaching the agonised beauty of perfect pleasure, which left her skin and her nerves and her muscles and even her bones a livened, quivering, warm liquid heap.

And his kiss this time lingered, his arms the tower of strength she clung to as he slowly brought her back to earth. I will never be able to let another man do this to me, she thought hazily, and had no idea that she'd whispered the thought out loud.

She only knew that something made him begin the whole, long, sensual journey all over again. They spent the whole afternoon like that—making love. They did not dress. They did not leave their room. They showered together and lazed together and stroked and kissed and made love together and eventually slept together in an intimately relaxed tangle of limbs.

CHAPTER NINE

HE WAS STRANGE, Lizzy found herself thinking again, as she watched Luc stand out in the hot sunlight deep in discussion with one of the island farmers, while she sat on the shady porch of a tiny blue-painted farmhouse, sipping at a tall glass of something cool and slightly odd-tasting the farmer's wife had brought out for her to quench her thirst.

He had three definite settings as far as she had been able to work out in the two weeks they'd been on the island. Cool and sophisticated, as on the couple of occasions he'd condescended to let her into the company of friends he had here. Or serious and deep, as he was being now while he listened intently to what the farmer was explaining to him. Then there was so hot and passionate she'd sometimes wondered if she was going to survive the demands he made on her body and her senses. Especially in the warm dead of night when he would wake her up because he needed her there and then with no space given for her to refuse.

If she could refuse, which she'd discovered she couldn't.

She was hooked on Luciano De Santis, she mused satirically as her eyes drifted over his wide shoulders pressed against the white of his tee shirt that hugged his torso all the way down to the narrow band of his cargo shorts. Naked, he was—colossal. Dressed, he was just too sexy to be real, even in a pair of baggy knee length shorts that had seen better days.

The old sting set up its usual flurry low in her abdomen as she slid her gaze down what was left on show of his long tanned legs. A man's legs, she observed. Strong and sturdy, peppered with dark hair and tightened by the muscular formation she knew for a fact was capable of crushing her in two.

Moving her eyes all the way back up him again, she saw the slight twitch he gave with his shoulders and knew he knew she was looking at him. It was like that between them now—a constant awareness that flowed across space like a magnetic vibration. Taking another absent gulp at her odd tasting drink she wondered if it all would still be there once they returned to reality the day after tomorrow.

Milan, not her other comfort zone on the shores of Lake Como. The real world in which Luc would slip back into his busy life and she would...

The chain of her thoughts stopped right there because she didn't know what she was going to do. She didn't know what they were going to go back to. Luc had kept the real world out of their time here, probably because he too was unsure himself as to what to expect out there.

She didn't even know if Bianca and Matthew had reappeared. She hadn't spoken to her father at all—hadn't wanted to and Luc hadn't encouraged her to ring him. And after their altercation about their wedding picture on their first day here she hadn't bothered to bring up the subject again because— well, she'd discovered that she preferred to pretend that all of this was the true reality and out there was the fantasy.

He turned to look at her then, so deliciously gorgeous she

felt her heart squeeze to an aching standstill. He'd been in an unusually sober mood all day, and that mood still reflected in the golden eyes he lowered to the half drunk glass in her hand, then lifted back to her too expressive eyes.

I love you, she was thinking, and just hoped to goodness he couldn't read *that* as he walked towards her, the farmer having been distracted by his mobile phone.

'Would you mind if I finished that for you?' He took the glass from her without waiting for an answer and downed what was left of the drink before she could tell him that the farmer's wife had prepared a glass full for him too.

Beautifully polite and arrogantly insolent all in one sexy package, she thought as she watched him grimace as if the drink had tasted odd to him too.

He had taken her everywhere with him during the last fortnight. She'd met very rich friends and very poor farmers and to a man they'd all treated her the same way, with warm smiles and welcomes that reflected their feelings for him—and his grandmother, since everyone had also commented on how much she looked like the late Contessa De Santis.

The farmer's wife came out on the porch and started chatting to him in Cajun while Lizzy sat and listened. She didn't care that she couldn't understand a word they were saying, she just loved to listen to the attractive dip and flow of their voices—especially Luc's.

'How many languages do you speak?' she asked him later as they drove away in the open-top sports car with her pink hat firmly in place on her head.

'I don't know,' he answered casually. 'I pick languages up easily.' He added a throw-away shrug as if it didn't mean a lot.

But it did mean a lot. It *said* an awful lot about him. He

was the true international high-flying businessman, cultured, educated, refined—supremely comfortable inside his own skin. Curling her legs beneath her on the seat, she turned to study his honey-gold profile, a smile playing with her mouth.

'What?' he said, turning a glance on her.

'Arrogant,' she murmured.

'I thought we had already established that.' He looked back at the road again.

'Conceited, then, if you think it's okay to shrug away the fact that you're fluent in a million languages.'

'A million?' He sent her a sexily lazy grin. 'You have a quaint way of offering me a compliment, *cara*. And you have your own amazing talents.'

'Like what?' Lizzy scoffed. 'Wearing hair-clashing hot pink because you like it?'

'That is certainly one of them.' He nodded with a grin. 'Then there is your talent for being quiet and unobtrusive when we are with other people, which only adds to your air of mystique.'

'Mystique?' Lizzy grimaced. 'I'm just shy, you know that.'

'Except with me…' the sunlight glossed his dark hair as he sent her a grin '…which is when another of your amazing talents puts in an appearance—the wildly passionate and sometimes downright provocative you, like you're being now.'

'I am not being provocative!' Lizzy protested.

'What would you call the way you are sitting there curled in that seat like an innocent kitten when you know your skirt has ridden up to the tops of your thighs?'

'You have a one-track mind.' She tugged the skirt down.

'You make sure that I have. And,' he went on without any noticeable alteration in his tone to warn her as to what was

coming, 'you have another amazing talent that really impresses
me because I don't know another person who can knock back
more than one mouthful of Martha's rum punch and still walk
a straight line, never mind have a sensible conversation.'

Lizzy's eyes widened and her mouth dropped open only
to close again when her tongue made a searching curl of the
taste buds inside her mouth. 'So that was the odd taste I
detected?'

'Martha's very own home-made rum.' He nodded. 'Now I
am sitting here driving the two of us back to the house as
quickly as I can so I can get you into bed before the full effect
kicks in.'

'Rum,' Lizzy repeated, and even as she did she felt the first
worrying stirrings begin to seep into her blood. She'd had rum
once before—and only once because the effect Luc spoke
about had been so—

'You are not coming anywhere near a bedroom with me,'
she said, straightening out her legs and sitting up straight.

'But we had such a fabulous time, *cara*,' he taunted softly,
'with you losing touch with all your inhibitions and me
gaining the sweet benefits of it.'

'It didn't taste like the rum I had that time.' She frowned.

'There is light years in difference between carefully refined
rum set down for decades before it is bottled, and the kind of
rum Martha makes,' he informed her. 'The first has the same
fine quality of the best French cognac, the other is more like
a witches' brew—slow to work but lethal once it gets going.'

'You drank half my glass,' she reminded him.

'Mmm,' was all he said, but Lizzy understood exactly
what the lazy *Mmm* was meant to represent.

Sure enough she couldn't get her legs to support her when

she tried to get out of the car. Luc laughed as he came around the car and gathered her into his arms and kept on laughing as he carried her into the house. She was already tasting his throat as if her life depended on it, her arms like two slender snakes around his neck.

'You taste of De Santis,' she mumbled luxuriously.

'I will take that as another compliment.'

'Mmm,' she responded and licked.

The bedroom door fell open, he carried her to the bed and dumped her on it, having to tug her clinging arms from around his neck so he could turn back to shut the door. By the time he turned again she was already half naked, kneeling in the centre of the bed like a mermaid floating on a sea of white linen.

'You've got too many clothes on,' she complained as he walked back to her.

'You think I don't know this?'

He lost his clothes while she wriggled her top off, set her breasts free from her bra, then arched her body in a fine, lithe stretch.

'I feel so sexy I want to crawl all over you.'

'Later,' he muttered, climbing on the bed and catching hold of her to lift her up, then bring her down again so she straddled his thighs in a warm blending of soft womanliness and strong, hard male.

Her arms went around his shoulders again, her mouth already searching out his, and she moved her hips against him until she caught the thrust of his erection just where she wanted it, her quiver of pleasure making him gasp, the firm clasp of his hands to her slender ribcage there to support her so she could set her own sensual pace.

And she rode the road of pleasure without a single care

that she groaned and gasped and even laughed, it was so glorious. She strung out the sweet agony for so long it almost hurt when she finally fell over the edge.

'If you ever drink rum in the company of others I will shoot you,' Luc muttered into her hair as he held her limp body against him.

But all Lizzy could do was whimper because, 'I want you again already.'

Passion was everything in paradise, Lizzy concluded much later when she lay stretched out on her stomach with her eyes closed and feeling as if there wasn't a cell in her body that hadn't been rejuvenated.

Luc came out of the bathroom—she picked up the clean scent of his recent shower. When he came to stretch out beside her and ran his fingertips up the length of her spine she smiled. 'I think you're gorgeous and sexy and a fabulous lover,' she told him.

'And I think you are still intoxicated,' he countered dryly, 'which means that later, when you recall saying all of that to me, you are going to hate yourself.'

'Not good for your ego,' Lizzy agreed—then, 'Oh,' she breathed, 'do that again—it felt just wonderful.'

But he didn't. Instead Luc rolled onto his back and stared at the ceiling, his mood suddenly sombre again. 'Elizabeth,' he said quietly, 'I need you to concentrate for a moment because I have something I have to tell you…'

When she made no response he turned his head to look at her, his mouth easing into a grimace when he realised that she was asleep. The alcohol-induced sensuality he had been enjoying for the last few hours having now dropped her like a stone into a deep, restful stupor.

He sighed, and went back to staring at the ceiling. The news he'd picked up on the internet this morning and put off telling her all day was going to have to wait a little longer.

A little longer, however, was swallowed up by the speed of events.

Lizzy came awake to find herself alone in the bed—if she didn't count the heavy thump taking place in her head. Rum, she recalled, the tender ache of her muscles as she dragged herself into the shower reminding her of how her afternoon had been spent.

The moment she went to look out of the window while she combed the damp tangles out of her hair she knew something was different. She could see two men pacing the sugar-soft sand on the beach and it only took a second for her to realise that they weren't just pacing, they were patrolling.

Losing the comb, she turned and walked out of the bedroom. Two harried looking maids passed her on her way down the stairs. They murmured hurried greetings as they continued upwards and their normal smiles were missing.

Puzzled and curious, she continued down into the hallway, following the sound of Luc's voice sounding grim and terse. She found him in the small dining room, standing by the table pouring coffee into a cup while he talked on his mobile phone.

He was dressed in the same shorts and tee shirt he'd stripped off so hastily earlier, but other than that everything else about him had changed. The stern look on his face, the sharp clip to his voice, even the way he moved was sharper, as if he'd switched on a fourth setting—that of grimly focused, fully charged, alpha tycoon.

'What?' she demanded the moment he turned to look at her, catching her first step into the room.

The mobile phone snapped shut, he tossed it onto the table. 'Our hideout has been discovered,' he told her without bothering to dress it up at all. 'Elena Romano decided it would be good fun to publish it on the internet, with a charmingly acid piece about the softer side of Luciano De Santis.' He grimaced. 'Your pink hat put in an appearance, via a photograph she must have taken as we walked away from her that day.'

'But—why would she want to do that now, almost two weeks later?' Lizzy frowned as she walked forward.

'Fabio has thrown her out,' Luc enlightened her. 'He caught her in a—comprising situation, apparently, with one of his deckhands. I presume she decided to use her meeting with us to divert media attention away from herself.'

'And has she?' Lizzy had reached the table.

'Yes.' Luc handed her the cup of coffee he'd just poured. 'The media mob is piling onto the island as we speak, which means that we are going to cut our stay here short.'

When he said short, he meant short, Lizzy realised a few seconds later when a helicopter swung over the top of the house and landed on the lawn by the pool. Walking across to the window to watch it settle, Lizzy saw just how efficiently Luc had thrown a ring of security around the property—tough-looking men had been stationed everywhere her eyes drifted.

'Is all of this really necessary?' she said with a cold little shiver.

'Yes,' he responded, his voice deep and tight. 'I have other news,' he said then, and waited for her to look at him before he added, 'The runaway lovers have re-emerged. Bianca is at Vito Moreno's home in Sydney, your brother is back in England.' There was a pause in which Lizzy held her breath because she could tell from the gravity of his expression that something bad was coming. 'He was arrested at Gatwick airport and is currently being interviewed by the police.'

She went pale. 'But I thought you said you had—'

'He confessed, *cara*,' Luc cut in grimly. 'He made a voluntary confession about taking the money from Hadley's and blew my cover-up to bits. Now I am expected in Milan to explain myself. We leave here in ten minutes.'

Ten minutes to get ready to leave was nothing to the nine long hours it took to fly back to Milan. Luc wasn't talking. He'd withdrawn behind a wall of icy courtesy, and Lizzy couldn't blame him. His pride had been hit, his integrity. Lizzy didn't think he was ever going to forgive any of them for it.

And the only slither of comfort she could glean from it all was that Matthew's arrest had not leaked out into the public arena. Luc spent most of the flight on the telephone working to ensure that it remained that way.

They arrived at Linate airport early in the morning to dark clouds and heavy rain. A limousine with blackened windows picked them up and transported them into Milan.

Luc remained on the phone throughout that journey too, the monotone flow of his voice never tiring, though Lizzy had switched off from it hours ago.

Half an hour later they were in his Milan apartment. Luc was checking his mail. Lizzy moved off, looking around her, aware that he was watching her, his eyes flicking her glances between reading the envelopes. He knew as well as she did that this was it—the hard reality of their marriage kicked in right here.

And as if to punctuate that he was wearing a suit, the first suit she'd seen him wear in two whole weeks. It was a smooth and elegant dark suit that enhanced just about everything about him from the breadth of his shoulders to the length of his long legs and even the sleek-styled darkness of his hair.

'I will show you around in a minute,' he murmured.

Lizzy turned to offer a fleeting smile. 'I've been here before.'

Then she turned away again. Even his voice sounded different, quiet and level and—cool.

The one time she'd been here—to a party he'd given the first week she'd been in Milan—his voice had sounded like that. And he'd worn a suit, something designer-cut to look casual. He'd moved through his guests with the smooth, silent grace of a satellite circling outer space. He'd barely noticed her in the crush—though he did pause to speak to her once, she remembered. *Ciao, how are you? Having a good time?*

Did he even remember her name?

Then she smiled because of course he'd remembered it. He was the man with a million languages logged in his brain, so one small name wasn't going to escape him.

'We will be spending most of our time here, so feel free to change anything you don't like.'

Lizzy nodded and moved through a wide opening into the vast cutthroat stylishness of the lounge. What was there to change? she mused as she wandered over to the window to check out the view. The pure silk grey curtains with that dramatically simple dark brown line threaded through them, or the matching cushions tossed so perfectly casually against scrumptious brown leather?

She could throw chintz at it all, she supposed—just to irritate his very good taste—or change a painting or two and put up some of her own rough sketches done in bold strokes of charcoal during one of her crazy moods that had used to erupt without warning when being quiet and placid had got on her nerves.

She turned away from the window, to find him standing in the opening through to the hallway. His expression was—unreadable, she decided described it best. Gorgeous, she allowed, as in gorgeously handsome and gorgeously tanned and even gorgeously unreadable.

'Can I have my own room?' Lizzy didn't even know she was going to say it until the words left her tongue.

'Own room as in what kind of room?' he came back smoothly.

Own room as in I don't want to sleep with you any more, she thought, but was so shocked by the discovery she didn't say it out loud. Instead she shrugged. 'My own bit of space.' She hedged for a compromise because she was going to have to seriously think about the other thing before she dropped that kind of bombshell. 'Somewhere I can put all my junk when I get it delivered.'

'You like junk?' He raised a curious eyebrow, but it wasn't really curious—it knew what it was she was hedging around.

So she nodded, pressing her lips together because they'd started to tremble and she could feel the threat of tears stinging the back of her throat. There was a great yawning gap opening up between them, which had nothing to do with the length of the room. And she was suddenly intensely aware of the age difference between them, the twelve long years that gave him the control to stand there and look beautifully at ease with what he was about to face, while she—

Lizzy swallowed. Her heart was pumping oddly, heavy and thick, because she knew that the yawning gap had started to widen the moment the helicopter had landed on the lawn in the Caribbean.

It had stretched even wider during the long, grim journey and then wider again when he'd come out of the bedroom on the plane just before they had landed dressed like that, and quietly suggested that she might like to change.

So here she was, standing in a neat pale grey suit that had somehow appeared without her knowing how on a hanger behind the bedroom door. And she felt like a stranger—to herself—a person carefully fashioned to suit *his* image when really she was—

'What's wrong, *cara*?' he prompted huskily and the tears in her throat almost beat her up in their rush to reach her eyes.

'Nothing,' she managed, though she didn't know how she managed it. 'I just feel strange here—out of place.'

'You will get used to it.'

Reassurance or an order?

'It's the—'

The telephone began to ring then, sounding so shockingly shrill after weeks without hearing one that both of them started in surprise. Luc went to answer it, striding back through the opening and across the hallway. Lizzy tried to pull herself together and followed him. He was standing in what looked like his study with the door swinging open wide. She diverted towards the back of the apartment where she re-membered the kitchen was situated and made herself busy hunting down the necessary things needed to make a pot of coffee.

When she heard him come in the room, she didn't turn to look at him. 'I have to go out now,' he told her.

She nodded, pressing her lips together again because she

wanted to say something about Matthew and the whole wretched mess her family had placed him in, but she just couldn't seem to find the right words.

'I don't know when I will be back, but I have arranged for an employee of mine—Abriana Tristano—to come here to—advise you as to how to respond to any fallout that may occur.'

'Like a PA?' she turned to ask him.

He nodded. 'She's good. Let her take care of everything. She has my mobile number to liaise with me if she needs to—clarify anything.'

I don't like this, Lizzy thought, standing there looking at him. 'I w-would prefer to come with you,' she said. 'Be seen at your side.'

He smiled for the first time in hours and hours, one of those sensually amused, very intimate smiles that softened the harshness out of his face, and it swam through her blood as potent as Martha's home-made rum.

'*Amore*, having you by my side will be too much of a dis-traction—as will coming over there and kissing you for sug-gesting it.'

Lizzy moved, she just had to do. 'Then I'm coming to you,' and she covered the space between them, lifting her slender arms around his neck so she could give him the dis-tracting kiss whether he wanted it or not.

He tasted warm like the man of the Caribbean, and smelled expensive like the man of Milan. When he didn't pull away and even slid his hands beneath her jacket to mould her against him, the silly uncertainties she'd brought with her into this apartment melted away.

'Don't let them bully you,' she murmured as their lips re-luctantly separated.

'You see this happening, with me?'

No, she was just delaying the moment when he walked away from her and her liquid grey eyes told him so. 'I'm just scared,' she confessed on a husky whisper.

'Don't be.' He touched his lips to hers again. 'I know what I'm doing.'

The doorbell pealed then, and he moved away from her. As she watched him stride down the hallway she saw the change take place in his whole mood and manner as the man from the Caribbean was cleared away.

Abriana was nice, though Lizzy had been ready to dislike her. She arrived wearing jeans and trainers and armed with fresh pastries from the local patisserie. Her warm, friendly nature kept Lizzy's anxieties damped down to a minimum. And she dealt firmly with every phone call and visitor that tried to gain entrance into the apartment.

It took twenty-four hours for Lizzy to realise that she'd been carefully isolated again, much as she'd been at the Lake Como villa. And she was being carefully protected from this new wave of media interest that had hitched its wagon onto their lives.

No phone calls, no newspapers for her to read what was being said, but even Luc couldn't stop the television from re-porting on the burning question—had Luciano De Santis, President of the De Santis Bank, misused his position of power in connection with a loan given to his father-in-law?

'Luc advised you not to watch this,' Abriana said worriedly when she saw Lizzy turn pale. 'He did not do anything wrong. He used his own money, not the bank's money, and he has clear proof of that.'

'Yes,' Lizzy said, trying—trying to believe what Abriana

was saying, but she knew more than Abriana did, just as she knew that Luc would not be called to answer questions if it were as neat and tidy as Abriana said.

She hardly saw him during the next long week. Although he came home to the apartment each night it was late, and he was tired and uncommunicative. As the days crawled by she watched the strain of it all inch tension lines into his face.

And he didn't sleep in her bed. He said it was because he didn't want to disturb her when he retired very late and got up so early the next day, and she understood that—she did.

But she missed him, meanly and selfishly she missed him and almost welcomed the miserable fact that she did.

Then, one week after they arrived back from the Caribbean, the feel of the mattress moving beside her brought her swimming up from a fitful sleep. By then a familiar pair of hands was taking hold of her and turning her into the burning heat of his hungry kiss.

The moment he let her up for air she searched his face through the semi-darkness. He looked different, relaxed, the strain and the tough self-control had gone.

'It's over?' she asked.

He nodded, levering himself up on his side so he could look down at her. 'Your brother is off the hook because the bank has decided not to press charges since the money went missing for only twenty-four hours,' he said. 'And your father simply told the truth and maintained he knew nothing about any of it.'

'And you?' she asked.

'I talked my way out of it,' he answered, 'By deciding on my story and sticking to it. So long as I continued to insist I knew nothing about the five and a half million your brother took, they could prove no wrongdoing on my part.'

Lizzy lifted a hand to touch her fingers to the rueful twist at the corner of his mouth. 'But what you did was—wrong?'

He didn't answer for a moment, his eyes dark on her anxious expression. Then he took hold of her fingers and kissed them.

'Morally, yes,' he said.

Tears spread like a film across her eyes. 'I'm sorry, then, that you felt you had to do something wrong for my benefit, but—thank you,' she added. Then, because she knew she just had to say it, in fact she'd been burning to say it throughout the long, hard week, 'I love you, Luc,' she whispered to him.

It was the first time she had allowed herself to say it and even hearing it fall from her lips set her heart pounding in her chest because she knew she couldn't lay herself more open to him.

Yet he said nothing—nothing for ages, just continued to kiss the tips of her fingers and look down at her through those dark golden, utterly unreadable eyes of his.

Then he smiled. 'Loving gratitude from my worst critic,' he mocked lightly. 'It was almost worth it.'

It was like receiving a kick in the teeth. Lizzy tried to get up, but he stopped her.

'No,' he husked, 'forget I said that. I'm still stinging from being forced to explain myself and that was unbelievably generous of you.'

Was he trying to make her feel better? Because he wasn't succeeding. She felt broken in two.

'And I love you too, *bella mia*,' he added huskily. 'Of course I do. Why else would I put my reputation at such risk if not for the woman I love?'

Why else indeed? Lizzy thought bleakly. Desire? Anger? Wounded pride? A determination not to look the fool Bianca had turned him into, no matter what it cost him?

She could have made the list grow and grow, if he'd let her, but, 'Now all I want is you, so badly I ache,' he roughed out, and the warm crush of his hungry mouth took away her ability to think.

For the first time since their wedding night they made love with a grim, silent intensity that pounded her wounded emotions and left her satiated but with tears on her cheeks.

He gently licked them away and said nothing. He continued to hold her close and said nothing. And when she woke the next morning he had gone from their bed leaving her with an ache that dragged on her insides.

It was an ache that was not going to go away any time soon, and indeed was about to become a whole lot worse.

Though Lizzy didn't know that when she crawled out of the bed that morning. In truth she would have preferred to remain in it, with her face buried in the pillow and the covers pulled up over her head. She did not want to face whatever the new day was bringing, but Abriana was due to arrive and she needed to get herself together by then.

There was a note waiting for her when she walked into the kitchen. It was propped up against the kettle and her fingers trembled as she picked it up and read Luc's precise bold scrawl. 'Dinner at eight' he had written. 'I will book a table somewhere special. Wear something fabulous. It will be our first date.' And he'd signed it, '*Ti amo*, Luc.'

Ti amo, Luc…

Thick tears crushed the muscles in her throat as she stood there trying to deal with the impact the endearment was having on her.

Ti amo, Luc…

She wished he hadn't written it. She wished with all of her

aching heart that he'd just pretended the words hadn't come up between them so she could try—try to forget how stupid she'd been and maybe manage to move on.

But *'Ti amo, Luc,'* told her he was feeling bad about his reaction to her when she'd said it. *'Ti amo*, Luc,' said he was attempting to make amends. *'Ti amo*, Luc,' reminded her that they had a marriage to continue whatever else had happened and *'Ti amo,'* was, she supposed, a basic part of it, even if it was offered without the sincerity of truth.

She crushed the note in her fingers and wrapped her slender arms tight around her aching ribs. The phone began ringing out in the hallway. It took six long echoing rings before she could bring herself to answer it.

'Yes?' she whispered.

'Elizabeth?' Luc questioned sharply. 'Why are you answering the telephone? Where is Abriana?'

Why was he the only person in the world who called her Elizabeth? she found herself thinking. Why did he have to be so painfully different from everyone else?

'Sh-she's not here yet,' she answered.

There was a buzzing silence. She wished she could think of something to say but she couldn't, and her voice was shaking—she'd heard it for herself when she spoke.

'Are you all right, *cara*?' he husked out then.

So he'd heard it too. Lizzy pressed her lips together. It was mad how one small endearment had the power to turn her into this much of a pained, quivering wreck. *Cara*, she could deal with. *Cara* was lightweight and familiar.

'Luc, I think I m-might catch a flight home to England today. Go and see—' she swallowed '—m-my father and—'

'The hell you will,' he bit out harshly, then followed it up with a blistering curse. 'What is the matter with you? Why are you choosing this moment in particular to do this to me?'

To *him*? She was doing it to herself! 'I just thought—'

'Well, *don't* think!' he rasped at her. '*Por Dio*, I will never understand women for as long as I live! I am on my way back to the apartment. You will do nothing until I arrive. We should not even be having this conversation! Abriana should be there to answer the damn phone!'

'Why are you on your way here?' Lizzy asked frowningly.

There was another sharp buzzing silence and she could almost see him seething inside his chauffeur-driven car. 'I will tell you when I get there. Our plans have changed. We will be going to the Lake Como villa. Use your time packing a suitcase for a stay there instead of packing one to leave me!'

The phone went dead. Lizzy stared at it in a state of blank disbelief. He never got angry—not fire-breathing angry, anyway. He preferred the icy kind that could freeze the blood in your veins.

The doorbell sounded its ring then. Replacing the telephone receiver, she went to let in her PA, with her head still whirling over too many things to make her stop and think before she turned the lock and opened the door.

The person she saw standing there dressed in unrelieved black sent her gasping in shocked disbelief.

'Bianca!' she breathed.

CHAPTER TEN

BURNING BLACK EYES spitting murder at her, Bianca Moreno took a step forward and threw her hand against the side of Lizzy's face.

'How could you, Lizzy?' she sizzled at her. 'How could you just marry him like that?'

The whip-crack sting sent Lizzy staggering backwards, her hand jerking up to cover her cheek. 'But y-you ran away with Matthew,' she stammered out. 'You left Luc—'

'I didn't leave him!' her best friend spat at her scathingly. 'Luc sent me away, because he said he'd found someone else and he didn't want to marry me any more!'

She was repeating her own press, Lizzy realized. 'But that isn't true. You know it isn't, you—'

Bianca stalked off, a shimmering mass of hurt tears and anger that Lizzy had to follow with her insides still shaking from the shock angry slap.

'Matthew rescued me.' She continued to use the press line from a tragic position in the centre of the living room. 'I called him up when I saw what was happening between you and Luc—'

'But nothing was happening!' Lizzy insisted.

'I needed Matthew to come and take you away before you ruined my life!' Swinging around to face her, Bianca let Lizzy see the pained tears in her eyes. 'He was going to do it too,' she said thickly, 'the very next morning after that—fiasco w-when I caught you and Luc together on the terrace. I saw your face, Lizzy! I knew what you'd been doing!'

The cringing guilt of that incident coming back to haunt her, Lizzy opened her mouth to say something, but nothing came out.

Bianca burned her a scathing look. 'I got you away from there as quickly as I could,' she went on. 'Your brother wanted to go to your room then and there and drag you home by the scruff of your traitorous neck, but it was already too late.' Her voice broke down into a choke. 'Luc arrived only minutes after we got back to the hotel. He told me it was over—right there in front of my cousin Vito and your brother, Lizzy!' she cried. 'He finished it between us and I have never been so humiliated in all of my life!'

None of this was true—not the way that Bianca was telling it anyway, but what Lizzy couldn't work out was why she was persisting in telling it to her as if it were!

'You know you're lying,' she husked out shakily.

'I'm lying?' Bianca seared out. 'Did you or did you not have the hots for my fiancé from the moment you set eyes on him?'

'Oh, God,' Lizzy choked in shuddering answer.

'We were friends—*best* friends! And you betrayed me in the worst possible way that you could! Well, now you're going to know what it feels like to be hurt beyond bearing and be humiliated, Lizzy, because I'm pregnant with Luc's baby and I want him back!'

With those final words ringing in the silence that followed, several things suddenly happened at once. Luc appeared tall and tense in the opening through to the hallway with Abriana standing white-faced at his side. Bianca saw him and on a broken sob she ran towards him and threw herself against his chest.

'I'm sorry, I'm sorry,' she kept sobbing over and over while she clung to him, and he just stood there with his handsome face cold like frozen marble and his golden eyes fixed on Lizzy's face.

He had to have heard what Bianca had said because she'd been shrieking loud enough to drown out the sound of him coming into the apartment. And he wasn't denying it could be possible. He wasn't pushing Bianca away. He was just looking at Lizzy—looking as if waiting for *her* to say something, but what was there for her to say?

And, anyway, it was as if someone had just switched on a light to make her see reality for the first time in weeks of self-denial. It was crazy and she knew it, but not *once* had she so much as considered that Luc and Bianca would be lovers. She'd just blocked the now sinkingly obvious out. Having to face it now, though, having to stand here with Bianca's finger marks still stinging her cheek and her stark eyes fixed on Luc's sternly controlled expression—glass case or not—she knew she was going to have to get out of here as fast as she could before she threw up.

Bianca was still sobbing into his chest as Lizzy managed to get her shaking legs to walk forward. She was vaguely aware that he'd muttered something at Abriana because she disappeared out of sight and the growing horror of it all throbbed like an invisible monster in the air surrounding her. The closer she came to them, the worse the throbbing felt.

When she finally drew level with them, Luc snaked a hand

out and caught her shoulder. She shuddered so violently he
bit out a curse.

'*Don't,*' he said in a dark husky rasp.

She paused to look at him, then at Bianca held against him,
then back into his eyes, and a strained, pale, helpless smile
twisted her quivering lips at the tableau they made—the man,
the jilted betrothed, the wife.

Maybe he was reading her mind again because Luc moved
his hand on her shoulder as if he was trying to use it as plea.
'*Don't,*' he said again. 'I will deal with it.'

Deal with it…Thick tears wrapped themselves around her
throat. For what was there for him to deal with? A near-hys-
terical ex-betrothed? A stung and stunned and stupidly naïve
wife? Or a baby, which totally, utterly overwhelmed the im-
portance of everything else.

She shrugged off his hand and walked away from him.
Hidden away inside the bedroom, she found herself staring
at her own image reflected back at her from the full length
mirror hung on one of the wardrobe doors. It was like looking
at a stranger, a long and curvy total stranger with grey eyes
and chestnut-coloured hair and an errant curl that insisted on
flopping over her brow.

It was over. It had to be. It didn't matter any more if most
of what Bianca had screamed at her was the detailed fabri-
cation put out there to save Luc's face. What mattered was
the child Bianca claimed that she carried.

The first De Santis heir.

She was the infiltrator in this little trio, Lizzy told
herself, which meant that she was the one who was going
to have to leave.

Maybe Bianca was right and she did deserve what was

coming to her. She certainly felt that she did as she carefully turned away from the mirror only to find herself staring at the bed. Then with a race-quick spring of nerve-dragging agony the panic erupted, the desperate need to get out of here now—while she could!

It took very little to do it, she realised painfully as she turned to yank open the closet door and dragged out the first suitcase she could lay her hands on. What she flung into that suitcase showed no sign of logic. Nor did the way she suddenly diverted halfway through and pulled open the wardrobe door to snatch at the first outdoor garment she saw. It was a black linen jacket she had never worn before. She dragged it on over the white tee shirt she was wearing with a pair of denims, then hunted down her handbag and rummaged through it with tight, trembling fingers to check that her passport was still in it along with her credit cards, then, finding everything in order, she completely forgot about the half-packed suitcase and spun to open the bedroom door.

All was quiet in the hallway as she walked along it. Even Abriana was nowhere to be seen. And the door to Luc's study was shut tight into its housing, telling her that he must have taken Bianca in there.

Outside it was still raining—raining—raining. She waved down a cab and climbed inside. Linate airport was busy. It was always busy but she managed to get a seat on a flight about to leave for London. Three short hours later she was walking through the arrivals gate at Gatwick.

And the first face she focused on was her father's. Tears once again started to threaten. 'H-how did you—?'

'Luc called me,' he explained, then nodded his head at someone standing behind her.

Lizzy glanced round, then withered out a smile as she turned back to her father's sombre face. She had been followed from the moment she'd stepped out of the apartment, tracked every foot of the way here by one of Luc's security team.

She didn't know why her tears picked that moment to break, but she threw herself sobbing into her father's arms.

'It's all right, Lizzy, you're home now.' Her father patted her back awkwardly. They were not a hugging, sobbing kind of family. 'Let's go and find my car.'

They were halfway home before she asked about Matthew. 'He's okay,' her father said. 'If nothing else, he learned a few hard lessons in life with his crazy escapade, the main one being that taking something that doesn't belong to you might be exciting while it's happening, but there has to be a point where you accept you're going to have to pay.'

Was he talking about Matt stealing Hadley's money, or her stealing Bianca from Luc? Lizzy didn't ask the question because she didn't want to know the answer.

'Where is he now?' she enquired instead.

'In one of those expensive rehab clinics paid for by Luc— didn't you know?' he said to her gasp of surprise. 'I thought Luc would have told you.'

If there was one thing Lizzy had taken away from her very short marriage it was that Luc only told her what he wanted her to know. 'Why rehab?' she questioned.

'Your brother had got himself into some messy stuff long before this thing with Bianca came up,' her father said grimly. 'I blame myself,' he added heavily. 'I should not have been so determined to make the two of you be the people I wanted you to be instead of the people you needed to be... Matthew owed a lot of money to a lot of unsavoury people,' he contin-

ued heavily. 'The idea of *borrowing* some of Hadley's loan
to pay these people was where the rest of his problems began.
One bad idea exploded into a damn foolish thirst for revenge
on me. The rest you know. He took off with Bianca for
Australia to learn his real lesson in life, that the greatest love
of your life is not always the sanest love of your life—as you
have no doubt just found out for yourself.'

Again Lizzy said nothing. She didn't want to think about
the insanity she had shown around Luc. All she wanted was
to walk back into her own home and into her old bedroom
and be miserable in there for the rest of her life.

Only it wasn't going to happen quite like that. The telephone was ringing even as they stepped into the house
through the front door. Her father picked it up.

'It's Luc,' he said, holding the receiver out to her.

But Lizzy just pressed her lips together and walked into the
kitchen. She didn't want to speak to him—probably ever again.

He rang again the next morning, and again she refused to
speak to him.

'We owe him a lot, Lizzy,' her father chided her cold stubbornness, grimly stretching out his hand and the phone.

'Not me,' she denied. 'I've paid my debt to him.'

The fact that she knew Luc must have heard her say that
didn't touch her at all because she had paid her debt to him
with kisses and heartache and by believing too many of his lies.

So where did he lie to you? a little voice in her head
challenged.

Stop it, she told it. Leave me alone with my complicated
misery. I like it. And she picked up her coffee-cup and took
it with her back to her lonely bed.

He didn't call again for the rest of the week and she hated

him for it. Hated and hated and *hated* him with a poison and a fierce vengeance so when he did finally turn up on the doorstep late one afternoon, she was more than ready to leap on him and hit him—just as Bianca had hit her.

Trouble was, you didn't lash out at a man who looked about as bad-tempered as Luc did, Lizzy accepted, unable to stop her eyes from greedily tracking over him from the top of his rain wetted head to the tips of his wet handmade leather shoes. He was wearing a long black woollen overcoat and like his hair and his shoes, it was speckled with its share of the rain that had been falling relentlessly across all of Europe for the last week, and the stern stark expression on his face was—tough.

'Can I come in?' he asked. 'And before you answer that,' he then put in darkly, 'let me advise you to remove that frosty pout from your lips, *cara*, or I might just decide to remove it for you.'

And he wasn't bluffing. Lizzy could see by the way he'd fixed the glinting gold of his eyes on her mouth that he was quite prepared to carry out his threat. And what was worse, she felt the burn, the old tempting vibration grind into action to spin out its link between the two of them. It brought her chin up, her eyes flashing out a green warning that clashed head-on with the gold.

'I don't know where you get off thinking you can just arrive here and start ordering me about,' she returned angrily, 'but let me tell you that you lost the right to—'

He took a threatening step forward, forcing Lizzy into taking a quick backward step. Her heart leapt, so did her breathing as six feet three inches of black-clad very grim male took the door from her clinging fingers, then replaced it on its latch.

Stifled by his closeness as his full intimidating presence filled the small hallway, Lizzy slid warily around him and walked into the living room and didn't stop until she reached the fireplace with its fire burning warmly in the grate.

He came to a halt in the doorway so they ended up facing each other across a twelve-and-a-half-foot gap.

The light was soft in here, the ceilings lower than those in his homes, so he suddenly looked taller and bigger, his face not quite as pale as it had looked on the doorstep a moment ago with the autumn cool to help blanch the colour out of it. And—tired, Lizzy noticed for the first time, the grim lines of tension he'd worn on his face throughout the week before Bianca had turned up well and truly back in place.

'You've lost weight,' he said, making her aware that while she had been studying him he had been doing the same thing to her.

'No, I've not,' she denied, but wrapped her arms around her body all the same as if they were going to disguise the pounds she knew she had dropped.

'And you look—tired.' He ignored her denial. 'Missing sleep over me, *cara*?'

'Oh, isn't that just typically arrogant of you to say that?' she snapped back.

To her surprise he grimaced, '*Sì*, probably.' Then with a sigh he lifted a hand up. 'May I remove my coat? It is— warm in here.'

Lizzy wanted to tell him that he wouldn't be staying long enough to bother, but in the end she pressed her lips together and nodded because—dear God, she didn't want him to go.

His fingers worked free the buttons and she watched every one of them separate from its buttonhole until the coat eventually came off. He was wearing a suit beneath it, another sleek dark suit that shrieked Luc in business mode and—

'Here, give it to me,' she said, walking towards him when he looked around for somewhere to put the wet coat.

Their fingers brushed as the coat exchanged hands, and he closed his around hers for a second—until she froze up like a statue and on a sigh he let go of her again.

Refusing to look at him, she took the coat out into the hallway. By the time she came back he was standing in front of the fireplace—more or less where she had been standing, only he had his back to her and his wide shoulders were rod straight and tense.

And the crazy, weak tears started to threaten the back of her aching throat because he was staring at a framed photograph of her taken at the age of eighteen when she had graduated from school. She was smiling, shy for the camera, that errant curl flopping over her brow. Bianca, had taken it. There had used to be another similar picture of Bianca but Matthew had removed it, her father had told her.

'How is she?' she asked thickly. 'Bianca, I m-mean.'

'She is well.' He turned to look at her. 'She's back in London with her parents. Elizabeth—'

'M-Matthew is out of rehab,' she quickly cut in.

'Yes, I know. Elizabeth—'

'He won't come home. This is a small market town where everyone knows everything about everyone and he just can't bring himself to face them all so he's staying with an old school friend in Falmouth… They're planning to take off round the world together—backpacking… He means to— find himself, and I suppose if anything good came out of w-what happened then it has to be that my father has accepted that he had been too tough on Matthew, so he's—'

'There is no baby, *amore*,' Luc quietly interrupted.

CHAPTER ELEVEN

LIZZY JUST STARED at him, her eyes like twin grey pools of blank incomprehension that made Luc grimace. 'I thought I would tell you before you ran out of innocuous things to say and resorted to telling me about the lousy weather,' he explained. 'Bianca *lied*, Elizabeth. She is not and never has been pregnant. She is just angry with everyone—you, me, your brother—angry with herself for making such a mess of her life…'

'You mean she—came to your apartment and said all of that just to hurt me?'

'And me.' He nodded. 'Though it has taken the full length of this miserable week to admit it.' His golden eyes glinted. 'She knows you well, *amore mia*,' he said softly. 'She knew just what to say to make you run from me. So now I am standing here wondering why it is you are still standing over there instead of throwing yourself at me in gratitude and relief!'

The sudden burst of his anger made Lizzy stiffen. 'G-grateful for what—?'

'That there is no child,' Luc elaborated. 'That I am not about to become involved in a heavy paternity suit and that you are still the woman I made my wife—and you should have stayed in Milan and supported me until this truth came out!'

And there it was, Lizzy realised, the reason why he had arrived here looking bad-tempered and tough. He was angry because she hadn't hung around to be mocked by everyone for a second time. He'd expected her to fall on him now he had given her the good news that it wasn't going to happen!

'You have a twisted sense of self-belief, Luc, if you truly expected me to fall on your neck with relief!' she informed him. 'Or have you forgotten I was already planning to leave you *before* Bianca put in an appearance?'

'I have forgotten nothing.' He moved, beginning to close the gap between them. 'I was merely giving you the opportunity to allow that small incident to fade quietly away.'

'Well, I don't want it to fade away,' she said, backing as he kept on coming, 'and don't you *dare* touch me!' she warned as she felt her spine hit the door. 'You've lied to me, bullied me, squeezed every last drop of feeling out of me, but what did you ever give me back?' she asked, a sudden onset of tears bringing him to an abrupt halt. 'Your wonderful body and the pleasure of using it is all that you gave back to me, Luc,' she informed him jerkily. 'And you dare to believe that that should be enough to keep me loyal and supportive to you?'

'No,' he sighed out, turning away from her to grab the back of his neck with a hand. 'You deserve better from me.'

And having him admit it did *not* make Lizzy feel better. 'Well thank you for that small crumb,' she said, wishing she were dead now because she just couldn't stem the sudden urge she had to throw herself at him anyway.

Then she remembered the note, the brief throw-away

'*Ti amo,*' and she threw herself round to drag open the living room door. 'That said, then I know you will understand that I w-would like you to leave now,' she said, hating the telling tremor she heard in her voice. 'My father will be home in a minute and I would prefer it if you—'

'No, he won't.'

Lizzy stilled in the doorway. 'Won't what?' she demanded.

'Be home soon,' Luc extended. 'He knows I am here,' he explained huskily. 'He thinks I am taking you out to dinner.'

'Dinner?' Her shoulders wrenched back. 'I don't want to have dinner with you.'

'It is the only way you will get rid of me, *cara,*' he said.

It was the cool way he relayed that that made her twist back to look at him. The moment she saw the way he was standing there looking as contained as hell, she knew he had turned back into the cool-headed Luc De Santis who did not play fair in a fight.

Tall, though, lean, sexily handsome. Lizzy found herself nervously moistening her lips. 'Explain that,' she instructed.

'Dinner,' he repeated. 'That is all. I have already reserved a table. All you have to do is to sit down with me and eat.'

Never in a million years was that all he was expecting her to do.

'Or I will call in your family debt...'

Ah, *now* he was talking, Lizzy thought. She understood this Luc so well! The unreadable expression, the arrogant tilt to his head that had once made her want to fly at him across the width of his desk.

'Dinner...' She folded her arms. The heavy sweep of his eyelashes dropped low as he watched her do it, and the tense quiver struck down her front. 'Where?'

'My hotel. I'm staying at Langwell Hall.'

Langwell Hall, Lizzy repeated silently. Only the best would ever be good enough for Luc. Langwell Hall was the finest hotel in the area—once a spectacular stately home left to go to ruin, now beautifully refurbished and transformed into a hotel.

And she knew exactly what he was doing with this oh, so polite, spiked-with-threat invitation; he was taking her out of her comfort zone here in her own home and putting them in the perfect place for him to feel comfortable in.

'I don't have anything fit to wear for dinner at Langwell Hall,' she informed him coolly.

Those gold eyes made yet another sensual dip down the front of her plain linen shift dress with its limp, shapeless shape. 'Come as you are,' he responded carelessly. 'We will be eating, not putting on a fashion show.'

And Lizzy was feeling angry enough to do it, resentful enough of his bullying tactics to just call his bluff and let him walk her into Langwell Hall's fancy dining room wearing a dress she'd had on for two days because she'd been too upset and depressed to bother changing it, but...

'Dinner,' she said again, with a different emphasis. 'That's *all*, then you bring me home again and leave with no more threats?'

'*Sì.*' He nodded—and he had to switch to Italian to make *his* emphasis.

Without another word she turned and walked into the hallway, chin up, eyes sparkling as she strode up the stairs to her room. Maybe she should have looked back because she might have caught the telling way he ran his palm over his face as if to wipe away the tension in it.

When she came back down again she was wearing a full-length black raincoat over the only half-decent dress she had here in England, which was a very modest knee-length matt-black jersey thing with long sleeves and a high neck.

Luc was already waiting for her in the hall with his coat back on and a sublime patience strapped to his face. His hire car was a Bentley Continental. It was like floating in luxury as they drove through the pouring rain.

They didn't speak. Like the dreadful calm before the violent storm, the static electricity played tunes on her nerves.

Langwell Hall lived up to all her expectations with its oak-lined and hushed great hall and grand oak staircase and its many reception rooms filled with beautiful old furniture, fine porcelain displayed in glass cases and its priceless works of original art.

They were shown to a table set into a corner of the elegant dining room. Someone invisible had taken their coats. Soft lamps instead of candles refined the atmosphere, sparkling crystal and polished silver and fine bone china graced the pure white tablecloths.

Luc waved the *maître d'* away to personally attend to Lizzy's chair. 'You need diamonds,' he murmured as he saw her seated.

'Not a good way to soften me up,' she drawled.

She was thinking of Bianca's diamonds. By the time he sat down opposite her she knew he was thinking about them too by the grimace she saw on his lips.

'Emeralds, then,' he recovered smoothly, 'to compete with your eyes.'

'That was corny,' she chided. 'And my eyes are grey.'

'Not right now, they are not,' he drawled softly, and smiled as the heat of an angry blush warmed her cheeks because they both knew her eyes only turned green when she was lost in the throes of heated passion.

Seemingly it didn't matter what kind of passion it was that was driving her.

The *maître d'* returned to offer Luc the wine list, but he just waved it away and ordered what he wanted. And because Langwell Hall was that kind of place, the order was taken with barely a glimmer of uncertainty that they could provide it. Menus were set down in front of them instead.

Lizzy opened hers and pretended to study it cover to cover. Luc just sat back and studied her.

'Stop it,' she said, without glancing up at him.

'I like looking at you,' he responded levelly. 'Sometimes you take my breath away.'

'Sex.' She named it dismissively.

'You want more than sex from me?'

That focused her attention, though not her eyes, on him; she kept them carefully lowered. 'My French isn't good enough to read most of this,' she murmured, indicating the menu. 'You are going to have to translate.'

'*Ti amo,*' he said. 'It means I love you.'

The way Lizzy jerked in response she almost knocked the glasses over. 'That was Italian.' Her eyes lifted, wide and wounded, to his. 'And don't make fun of me, Luc—' even she could hear the pained shake in her voice '—or I walk.'

But his face didn't wear a hint of mockery anywhere, neither did his sigh sound mocking as he reached into the inside pocket of his jacket, then leaned forward to place something down on her menu.

Needing to swallow the lump in her throat now because

his eyes were so dark and intent on her, Lizzy looked down—and froze.

'Tell me,' he said quietly then, 'which part of this note upset you so much that you screwed it into a tight ball and threw it to the kitchen floor.'

Lizzy shook her head, the tears gathering. 'I—didn't know I had dropped it there.'

'This part?' he persisted as if she hadn't spoken, point-ing with a finger at the bit where he'd written, 'Dinner eight o'clock.' 'This part upset you because you believed I was issuing one of my arrogant commands instead of a request? Or was it this part, *cara,*' he went on gently, 'where I was insensitive enough to point out it would be our first date?'

He knew which part it was that had upset her—he'd just teased her with it before he produced the evidence!

'I'm not playing this game,' she breathed and jerked to her feet.

He stood up also, catching hold of her wrist as she went to leave. *'Ti amo,'* he said.

'No,' she whispered and tried to pull free.

But his fingers tightened. *'Ti amo,'* he repeated yet again, tensely. 'I will keep saying it until you listen to me.'

'In the same way you made a joke of it in bed?'

It was out there in the dining room before she could stop it, her impulsive tongue throwing out the biggest hurt he had ever wounded her with. People stopped eating to look at them; the dining room fell deathly silent.

'I tried to put it right in this note.' He held her eyes with the burning intensity of his. 'I wrote it there because I wanted you to know that I meant it, but you saw it as just another sign of my twisted humour and arrogance.'

'You're the most insensitive brute on this earth,' Lizzy shook out at him.

'*Ti amo,*' he said again, deeply, doggedly. 'You tell me I am too old for you and I agree, yet still I blackmailed you and I married you and I want to stay married to you.'

'I'm the same age as Bianca—what's the difference?' She frowned irritably, picking out the only part of that she wanted to argue with.

The look on his face altered. He tugged until she landed in quivering shock against his chest. Opening her mouth to protest, she saw what was coming the quivering second before his mouth landed like a burning brand on hers. And it wasn't a quick demonstration of male desire either, it was hot and it was hard and it probed and seduced every dark corner of her mouth until she knew she would have fallen down if he had not been holding her up.

She barely registered the gasp that rippled through their captive audience. People—*refined* people—drinking in the sight of Luc De Santis making passionate love to his wife!

'That is the difference,' he husked when he eventually set her mouth free.

But Lizzy shook her head. 'You're a taker, Luc,' she whispered unsteadily. 'If I let you you'll just keep on taking and taking until there's nothing of me left. You were cruel that night, you know?' She threw her clenched, shaking fist at his chest. 'And you did it deliberately. You believe a quick note left propped up against the kettle was going to put that right?'

Someone somewhere murmured something. Lizzy turned her head; she saw the sea of faces looking at them. Her mouth wobbled, lips burning and pulsing, she released out a small sob, then broke free of him and just ran.

And she actually made it as far as the grand hall before he caught up with her and scooped her right off her feet. 'You can use your fists on me again in a minute,' he gritted out and she fought him. And he turned and headed for the lift.

One brave hotel employer dared to try and stop him. 'She's my wife,' he announced as if that meant everything. 'You don't come between a man and his wife!'

And he stepped into the lift.

The last image Lizzy carried with her as the doors closed on them was an unrestricted view across the great hall and into the dining room where everyone was on their feet and staring at them.

'I hope you enjoyed causing that awful spectacle!' she choked out. 'Now put me down!'

'Not in this life,' Luc responded. 'You refuse to listen. You are an unforgiving harridan. You don't care what you make me feel. You love me but you don't *love* me!'

It was a distinction that made Lizzy stop fighting him so she could try to work it out. The moment she relaxed in his arms he let her feet slither to the ground. The doors to the lift parted as if he'd planned it. And maybe he had, Lizzy wouldn't put it beyond his capabilities. He dragged her out by the clamp of fingers he had around her wrist. The slide of a plastic key and she found herself standing in the most palatial suite of rooms she had ever seen.

The door closed, she heard the lock hit home. At last he let go of her and walked away. He was stiff with anger, she could see it pulsing from every part of him. He hooked up a bottle of something, poured some into a glass and downed it in one swallow, then finally turned.

'What else do you want from me?' he demanded, spreading his arms open wide. 'I let Bianca go. I married you as soon as I could arrange it. I put my pride and my reputation on the line for you. How many hints do you need before you stop being blind and see why I did these things?'

Lizzy tried her best to make her dizzy head think clearly, but all it was doing was soaking up his tense posture, the streaks of dark colour across his cheeks. He was angry—yes. He was defensive—yes. He was tall and dark and unbelievably more gorgeous to her than ever because he was finally opening up—for her.

Her fingers made a fluttering gesture, then came together across her front beneath the point where her heart was rattling around in her chest like an overexcited pup.

'*Ti amo?*' she dared to ease out.

He tensed—all of him tensed, then he gave a curt nod of his head. 'From the first time our eyes met in London,' he admitted. 'It came as a severe shock to me. I thought it was because you reminded me so much of *nonna*, but the feeling did not go away and I wanted it to. My life was already mapped out. I was betrothed to Bianca—'

'And sleeping with Bianca,' Lizzy put in huskily.

'What do you want me to say?' he demanded heavily. 'I'm a thirty-four-year-old man and I did not embrace celibacy while getting to this age.'

'I didn't think you did,' Lizzy said stiffly. 'I just didn't—'

She stopped, taking a bite out of her bottom lip because she knew what she had been about to say sounded stupid and immature and totally unfair—but she just hadn't thought about Bianca with him in that way. She didn't even know why it should matter to her so much yet it did.

'With Bianca it was just—'

'Don't,' she choked, not needing to hear him compare the two of them as if they were—

'No,' he sighed, hunching his shoulders and turning away from her, his stance weary and bleak.

Then— 'No,' he said again and spun back to face her again. His chin jutted and his expression turned fierce. 'I am going to say it,' he insisted, 'because I think it needs to be said. Bianca and I were engaged to be married so of course we were intimate. This is the twenty-first century, *cara*, an age in which most women expect their relationships to be intimate! But the intimacy stopped when I met you,' he admitted. 'A fact which probably contributed greatly to Bianca taking other lovers.'

He saw Lizzy's shocked expression and smiled cynically. 'Our decision to marry had nothing to do with love, *cara*. Bianca was telling the truth when she called it forming a dynasty. She had the right name and she was beautiful.'

He paused, the words catching in his throat. 'But I made a big mistake,' he continued then. 'In my arrogance, when I didn't bother to look for the right woman because I believed I did not need to with Bianca there in the wings of my life, I did her no favours, or myself, by accepting what fate had handed to me on a plate. Then I met you and I was way too attracted to you to be fair to anyone. The way you just had to keep looking at me fascinated me. I watched for you doing it and arrogantly took it as my due without bothering to analyse why I liked to feel your eyes on me.'

His eyes blazed a golden trail across her pale, still face.

'Your hair fascinates me,' he murmured softly. 'I love its colour and the way it does its own thing and you don't care. I love your long, womanly shape and your soft, womanly curves and I miss you when you are not curled against me in our bed. I miss being able to fall asleep with my hand filled by the warm softness of your breast, or waking up with your mouth a brush away from my mouth and your hand claiming possession of *me*. You want to hear more?' he flicked out tautly.

Like a mouse mesmerised by the big jungle cat, Lizzy nodded.

'Okay,' he said and took in a deep breath. 'I *hate* the way I took your innocence. It plagues me constantly that I was so tough on you. I never want to see a look on your face like the one you wore when Bianca told you she was pregnant by me. And I *despise* that cheap excuse for a dress you are wearing because I can't see your beautiful figure through it and I *want* to see it. I want to lust after you even if you never let me touch you again. And I adore—' his voice softened and grew silky '—the way you're standing there lapping all of this up because you believe you deserve it when you *know* retribution is going to come at you for being such a greedy—' he took a step forward '—selfish, unforgiving woman with sex on her mind.'

'We don't have sex. We make love,' Lizzy corrected.

'Ah.' At last the strain relaxed from his face. 'So you admit you get the difference.'

Reaching up, he took hold of a fistful of her hair and tugged. Her head went back, exposing the length of her creamy throat to him and locking her eyes with his.

'Green,' he said. 'You're dying to rip my clothes off.'

'I want your baby,' she whispered.

And his golden eyes turned black, the studding power of the lion in him surging to the fore on a hot adrenalin rush as he dealt wih the rear zip to her dress.

The cheap black fabric fell away whilst her fingers were busy with the buttons on his shirt. He lost the jacket. Warm dark skin as taut as leather and clouded by dark virile hair brushed the backs of her fingers as she worked. She felt muscles flinch and flex as she worked.

And he didn't break contact with her eyes as she did it. He did not claim her waiting mouth. He just built on the pulsing sexual tension because—that was how they liked it, singing along wires pulled taut through the rushing heat of their blood.

His shirt was cast aside, her dress along with it. She unclipped her bra and discarded that too—and still they made no physical contact other than his fist in her hair and her hands now dealing with the clip and zip of his trousers.

But her lips had started to tremble and his eyes had gone from black to flames of burning gold. 'Take the shoes off yourself,' she tremored.

As he obediently heeled the first shoe off, one of her hands slid around his neck and the other slid inside his loosened trousers. Stretching up on tiptoe, Lizzy placed her lips against his ear.

'*Ti amo,*' she whispered and felt his response run like Martha's rum through his body. It raced along the place her hand was holding, and raged like fire across his face.

'*Ti amo,*' she whispered again across the burning temptation of his lips.

Then her hands squeezed—both of them, the one holding the velvet-smooth power of erection captive and the one clasped around his neck so she could bring his mouth into full, hungry contact with her own hungry mouth.

'I hope you appreciate you are going to pay for that,' he

muttered tensely when she pressed her teeth into his warm
bottom lip.

'Just something else I owe you,' Lizzy sighed mock tragi-
cally. 'Five and a half million kisses, a few De Santis cubs
and one sexy bite of your lip.'

'You will never pay me back in this lifetime,' he declared
confidently as he picked her up in his arms and walked through
to the bedroom and tumbled her down on some really
decadent-looking four-poster bed that knocked spots off the
one in the Caribbean because of its heavy drapes in a dark red
fabric and the matching cover that made her skin look so
pearly white and clashed so alarmingly with her corkscrew
hair.

But Luc loved what he was seeing—Lizzy saw it blazing
like golden fire in his eyes.

'I give you leave to try,' he invited as he stripped the rest of
his clothes off, then dealt with what else she had left on with the
cool economy of a man who knew how much he was exciting
the woman he was about to throw himself down on top of.

'Do I get to start soon?' she quizzed innocently.

'*Sì.*' He made the long snaking stretch with his body until
he completely covered her. 'I will keep an account.'

MILLS & BOON®
Pure reading pleasure

JULY 2008 HARDBACK TITLES

ROMANCE

The De Santis Marriage *Michelle Reid*	978 0 263 20318 9
Greek Tycoon, Waitress Wife *Julia James*	978 0 263 20319 6
The Italian Boss's Mistress of Revenge *Trish Morey*	978 0 263 20320 2
One Night with His Virgin Mistress *Sara Craven*	978 0 263 20321 9
Bedded by the Greek Billionaire *Kate Walker*	978 0 263 20322 6
Secretary Mistress, Convenient Wife *Maggie Cox*	978 0 263 20323 3
The Billionaire's Blackmail Bargain *Margaret Mayo*	978 0 263 20324 0
The Italian's Bought Bride *Kate Hewitt*	978 0 263 20325 7
Wedding at Wangaree Valley *Margaret Way*	978 0 263 20326 4
Crazy about her Spanish Boss *Rebecca Winters*	978 0 263 20327 1
The Millionaire's Proposal *Trish Wylie*	978 0 263 20328 8
Abby and the Playboy Prince *Raye Morgan*	978 0 263 20329 5
The Bridegroom's Secret *Melissa James*	978 0 263 20330 1
Texas Ranger Takes a Bride *Patricia Thayer*	978 0 263 20331 8
A Doctor, A Nurse: A Little Miracle *Carol Marinelli*	978 0 263 20332 5
The Playboy Doctor's Marriage Proposal *Fiona Lowe*	978 0 263 20333 2

HISTORICAL

The Shocking Lord Standon *Louise Allen*	978 0 263 20204 5
His Cavalry Lady *Joanna Maitland*	978 0 263 20205 2
An Honourable Rogue *Carol Townend*	978 0 263 20206 9

MEDICAL™

Sheikh Surgeon Claims His Bride *Josie Metcalfe*	978 0 263 19902 4
A Proposal Worth Waiting For *Lilian Darcy*	978 0 263 19903 1
Top-Notch Surgeon, Pregnant Nurse *Amy Andrews*	978 0 263 19904 8
A Mother for His Son *Gill Sanderson*	978 0 263 19905 5

MILLS & BOON®

Pure reading pleasure

0608 Gen Std LP

JULY 2008 LARGE PRINT TITLES

ROMANCE

The Martinez Marriage Revenge *Helen Bianchin*	978 0 263 20058 4
The Sheikh's Convenient Virgin *Trish Morey*	978 0 263 20059 1
King of the Desert, Captive Bride *Jane Porter*	978 0 263 20060 7
Spanish Billionaire, Innocent Wife *Kate Walker*	978 0 263 20061 4
A Royal Marriage of Convenience *Marion Lennox*	978 0 263 20062 1
The Italian Tycoon and the Nanny *Rebecca Winters*	978 0 263 20063 8
Promoted: to Wife and Mother *Jessica Hart*	978 0 263 20064 5
Falling for the Rebel Heir *Ally Blake*	978 0 263 20065 2

HISTORICAL

The Dangerous Mr Ryder *Louise Allen*	978 0 263 20160 4
An Improper Aristocrat *Deb Marlowe*	978 0 263 20161 1
The Novice Bride *Carol Townend*	978 0 263 20162 8

MEDICAL™

The Italian's New-Year Marriage Wish *Sarah Morgan*	978 0 263 19962 8
The Doctor's Longed-For Family *Joanna Neil*	978 0 263 19963 5
Their Special-Care Baby *Fiona McArthur*	978 0 263 19964 2
Their Miracle Child *Gill Sanderson*	978 0 263 19965 9
Single Dad, Nurse Bride *Lynne Marshall*	978 0 263 19966 6
A Family for the Children's Doctor *Dianne Drake*	978 0 263 19967 3

MILLS & BOON
Pure reading pleasure

AUGUST 2008 HARDBACK TITLES

ROMANCE

Virgin for the Billionaire's Taking Penny Jordan	978 0 263 20334 9
Purchased: His Perfect Wife *Helen Bianchin*	978 0 263 20335 6
The Vasquez Mistress *Sarah Morgan*	978 0 263 20336 3
At the Sheikh's Bidding *Chantelle Shaw*	978 0 263 20337 0
The Spaniard's Marriage Bargain *Abby Green*	978 0 263 20338 7
Sicilian Millionaire, Bought Bride Catherine Spencer	978 0 263 20339 4
Italian Prince, Wedlocked Wife *Jennie Lucas*	978 0 263 20340 0
The Desert King's Pregnant Bride *Annie West*	978 0 263 20341 7
Bride at Briar's Ridge *Margaret Way*	978 0 263 20342 4
Last-Minute Proposal *Jessica Hart*	978 0 263 20343 1
The Single Mum and the Tycoon Caroline Anderson	978 0 263 20344 8
Found: His Royal Baby *Raye Morgan*	978 0 263 20345 5
The Millionaire's Nanny Arrangement Linda Goodnight	978 0 263 20346 2
Hired: The Boss's Bride *Ally Blake*	978 0 263 20347 9
A Boss Beyond Compare *Dianne Drake*	978 0 263 20348 6
The Emergency Doctor's Chosen Wife Molly Evans	978 0 263 20349 3

HISTORICAL

Scandalising the Ton *Diane Gaston*	978 0 263 20207 6
Her Cinderella Season *Deb Marlowe*	978 0 263 20208 3
The Warrior's Princess Bride *Meriel Fuller*	978 0 263 20209 0

MEDICAL™

A Baby for Eve *Maggie Kingsley*	978 0 263 19906 2
Marrying the Millionaire Doctor *Alison Roberts*	978 0 263 19907 9
His Very Special Bride *Joanna Neil*	978 0 263 19908 6
City Surgeon, Outback Bride *Lucy Clark*	978 0 263 19909 3

MILLS & BOON®
Pure reading pleasure™

AUGUST 2008 LARGE PRINT TITLES

ROMANCE

The Italian Billionaire's Pregnant Bride *Lynne Graham*	978 0 263 20066 9
The Guardian's Forbidden Mistress *Miranda Lee*	978 0 263 20067 6
Secret Baby, Convenient Wife *Kim Lawrence*	978 0 263 20068 3
Caretti's Forced Bride *Jennie Lucas*	978 0 263 20069 0
The Bride's Baby *Liz Fielding*	978 0 263 20070 6
Expecting a Miracle *Jackie Braun*	978 0 263 20071 3
Wedding Bells at Wandering Creek *Patricia Thayer*	978 0 263 20072 0
The Loner's Guarded Heart *Michelle Douglas*	978 0 263 20073 7

HISTORICAL

Lady Gwendolen Investigates *Anne Ashley*	978 0 263 20163 5
The Unknown Heir *Anne Herries*	978 0 263 20164 2
Forbidden Lord *Helen Dickson*	978 0 263 20165 9

MEDICAL™

The Doctor's Bride By Sunrise *Josie Metcalfe*	978 0 263 19968 0
Found: A Father For Her Child *Amy Andrews*	978 0 263 19969 7
A Single Dad at Heathermere *Abigail Gordon*	978 0 263 19970 3
Her Very Special Baby *Lucy Clark*	978 0 263 19971 0
The Heart Surgeon's Secret Son *Janice Lynn*	978 0 263 19972 7
The Sheikh Surgeon's Proposal *Olivia Gates*	978 0 263 19973 4